AF444841
ONE NIGHT IN
Paris
A FRIENDS TO LOVERS STANDALONE ROMANCE
ADRIANA PECK

ONE NIGHT IN PARIS

A Friends to Lovers Standalone Romance

Adriana Peck

ISBN-13: 9798612792505
ISBN-10: 1477123456

Cover design by: Adriana Peck
Library of Congress Control Number: 2018675309
Printed in the United States of America

CONTENTS

ONE NIGHT IN PARIS
(*Une Nuit à Paris*)
A Novella

Adriana Peck

CHAPTER ONE

As I collect my carry-on from the overhead container and nudge my way towards the aisle, I realize I'm well and truly on my own for now. I've spent the last four months in an apartment with three other girls going to school in Berlin, our one semester studying away from the good old US of A. We travel together on the weekends, ready to see the sights together. Me, little Annie Thompson from Los Angeles, together with my best friends Chloe, Daisy and Samantha. The four of us together have traveling figured out. I'm the one who handles the tickets and reservations, Chloe handles the food, Daisy is the transit expert, and Samantha's just along for the ride. Our dingy apartment in downtown Berlin's managed to keep us in the center of the action as we peruse the city every night, looking for fun.

But this weekend, I'm alone. I've decided to take a round-trip of my own to Paris while Chloe, Daisy and Samantha take the weekend off to study. I don't need to hit the books. I'm doing just fine in all my classes, because unlike my three roommates I don't go boy-crazy every night in the clubs in Berlin. So I've got a weekend to myself, and I'm spending it in Paris.

I know I'll miss them all. Daisy with her one-liners that never seem to run out. Samantha and I can talk about *anything* together: books, sports we've never heard of before, flea market finds. And of course, I'm going to miss Chloe the most. We'd been best friends for years, ever since we were kids. But we drifted apart in college, going to separate schools until we suddenly found ourselves on this journey together, winding up as randomly-assigned roommates for the study abroad program we'd both signed up for independently. I can't believe how much I missed her, and how much we've grown apart since high school. This semester's been a great time for us to catch up. Every day we try to do something new. This weekend's something new, of course. Chloe's not here though. It's just me, alone, but I'm still ready and excited to see Paris for myself.

As I disembark the plane, I already find Charles De Gaulle Airport to be big and foreign and a little scary, if I'm being honest. I spent four years in high school and two in college studying German. I don't speak a lick of French, and, unfortunately for me, this airport is plastered in French text that I can't translate to save my own life.

I spot a sign that reads *SORTIE*. I pull out my phone and check my translation app I've been using when English or German isn't the language of the country I'm visiting. Sure enough, *sortie* means exit, so that's where I head. I don't have any checked luggage to pick up, only the clothes on my back and what little meager possessions I managed to stuff into my carry-on back in Berlin. I've got a ukulele, one I purchased when I arrived in Europe. I've been practicing on it every day since then. I've got some other things, too, a change of clothes, toiletries, and a spare novel by an old-timey science fiction writer. It's about a robot rebellion on Mars, I think. I haven't read too much of it yet. It's not much, but it's what I need to get around town for a weekend. And Paris is no ordinary town, that's for certain.

It's a clear blue afternoon in France when I leave the airport and step outside the revolving door. I take a deep breath. The air here smells of cigarettes, *reeks* of cigarettes, even. I wonder if it'll get worse when I approach the city itself. I look around, figuring I can catch a cab or find a bus station to take my to the heart of Paris where my hostel's waiting for me. All the cabs are already carrying passengers, however. Tired-looking cabbies load heavy suitcases in trunks for pretty ladies wearing elegant dresses. I recognize a swath of people from the same flight as me that departed Berlin. They're heading down a flight of stairs to what appears to be a parking garage, but the sign above the stairs reads METRO. I join them, pull out my phone to see what neighborhood my hostel is in. I'm supposed to get off at the *Gare du Nord* station. It's in an area that's really close to the Eiffel Tower, and looking at the Metro stops I find that same spot on the green line, heading north.

I take the green line all the way to the city. The metro's crowded when we all hop on at the airport, and with each passing stop more and more passengers disembark. By the time I can see the Eiffel Tower from my window, the passenger car only holds four other people besides myself.

The metro pulls to a stop, the announcer blares:

"*Gare du Nord.*" and I jump up, bag in hand as I disembark onto the Parisian cobblestoned street. The other passengers look to their smartphones and books for entertainment, but I'm content just looking around me as I take in the view of the city. Well, not the city yet. I get out at a train station that reeks of cigarette stench even worse than the airport. I was right. The smell *did* get worse when I entered the city.

As I step off the Metro and climb up the stairs out the station to the neighborhood above, I'm greeted by a hustling and busting part of town that appears to be a marketplace during a rush hour. The trees planted every few feet are in a bright orange-and-yellow fall bloom. Fruit vendors camp out underneath white-and-red striped awnings. Sharp-dressed waiters in button-down shirts carry trays of food out to restaurateurs sitting at tables outside. The shoppers in the market squeeze past one another, and they squeeze past me a little too aggressively. French-style gothic architecture decorates the buildings that stack above us, but never journey higher than four stories tall. I know there are skyscrapers when I track closer to the heart of the city, but for now I'm content with the quaintness of the neighborhood here. Compared to Berlin, it's a quiet day.

As I push my way past the crowded marketplace gatherers, I pull out my phone again to double-check the address of the hostel. The Dainty Paris Hostel is supposed to be one of the nicer places that's still within walking distance of the *tour Eiffel*. There are directions from the metro stop, too, but they're written in French. So I'm going to have to wing it, I suppose.

The first direction says something about going *nord* through

Rue Ambroise Paré, and I look around to see if there are any street signs. One of the first things you learn while studying abroad is the fact that the green-and-white street signs in America are not commonplace all over the world. A lot of European countries put the street signs on the sides of buildings, adjacent to the street for which they are named. I've gotten lost one too many times in a busting European city setting. I don't plan on that happening again.

On the corner where I stand, I can see three street signs, *Rue de Maubeuge*, *Place Napoléon III*, and *Rue de Compiegne*. I head down *Maubeuge* street, looking left and right as I cross the road to the other side where I know my hostel will be. It's supposed to be right between a bookstore and a pharmacy, and I know it's a few block walk from the metro stop. I find *Rue Ambroise Paré* soon enough, and I'm heading on the right street in the right direction toward my hostel.

Before I know it, I'm passing a library. There's a pharmacy just up ahead, I can see the red cross on the white background. My hostel must be just to my left, and I peer up and see the sign I've been hunting for ever since I disembarked from Charles De Gaul:

Dainty Paris Hostel. I'm here.

I go inside, check in with the front desk to complete my reservation. A kind-looking old lady with the poofiest white hair I've ever seen mans the counter. She greets me warmly in French, but after she sees my face of American confusion she laughs and switches languages. Her name tag reads Clara.

"Name, please, miss?" Clara the receptionist says with a very thick accent, struggling to force the words out. We laugh over the awkwardness of the situation and manage to meet in the middle speaking half-English, half-French with a little bit of German peppered in as I complete my reservation.

My room's been ready for a half-hour, and the four other strangers have yet to check into their bunks. I'm the first to arrive, so I pick whichever bed I want first as soon as I'm up the short flight of stairs that lead to my room. The top bunk closest to the door seems nice enough, so I take the key out of the locker and put my stuff in there, locking the safe tight as I put the key on my keyring for safekeeping.

Now I'm free to do as I please. I go back down to the front desk, where Clara the receptionist still mans her post. I figure if there's anyone who can give me a recommendation as to what I can do in the city, I'm sure I can't go wrong asking a local.

"Clara, what is the first thing I should do in the city?" I ask her slowly, in case she has trouble understanding my words.

"Eiffel Tower," she says with a wink. "Best in town. Best in the *world*."

I nod. Of course that's where I should go first. Clara pulls out a map of the area around the hostel. She takes a pen, draws a line from where we are now to the nearest public square. Then, her pen takes a sharp right and heads East.

"Just a few blocks after that and then you will find the tower," Clara explains kindly and slowly. She's probably done this spiel a million times before with Americans a million times ruder and more impatient than me, and I nod politely as she illustrates the steps I'll have to take to see one of the greatest architectural achievements ever erected by man.

And so, Clara-marked map in hand, I journey back outside in the Parisian cityscape, alone to my own devices without even a French to English dictionary to guide me.

At 20, I feel like I'm much more older now that I've been traveling on my own as I country-hop on weekends with or without my roommates. Sure, journeying together as a group has been more than rewarding. Chloe and I have become sorta-kinda best friends again, every time we travel together I make sure to take a picture with Chloe to send back home to our parents. We went to the same high school, after all, not the same college, but we still managed to find a way to study abroad with the same company, who were more than happy to put us in a room together with two other girls. Right now I find myself missing Chloe quite a bit. But she's got important studying to do. If she fails this semester, I know her Dad will probably kill her, she's said so herself. So, during my solo trip to France, I resolved to find a gift for Chloe that'll at least take her mind off of things until finals are over with in just under a month.

On my way to the Eiffel Tower I see a bright-green-and-purple awning that catches my eye. As I pass closer to the shop, I see a film reel that's been stenciled on the awning, and I nearly jump for joy. Chloe *loves* cinema, and we've shown a new movie to our roommates Daisy and Samantha nearly every night we've been in Berlin together. Chloe and I bonded over our shared passion of old black-and-white romance movies, so I pop inside to get Chloe her gift.

The movie shop's decked out from top-to-bottom, stacking DVD's and VHS's and whatever-color-Ray's from floor to ceiling. There's a crusty-looking old man behind the front counter, and in my mind I immediately want to ask him if he knows Clara from the hostel. Of course, I know they don't, but something in my American mind wants me to believe that all these old French people somehow know each other from years and memories past. It's much more romantic that way.

I ask the clerk if he speaks English.

"Yes, ma'am, I do," he smiles and says in a perfectly American accent. Fantastic. I tell him I'm getting a gift for someone who's hitting the books hard, and I ask him for the most obscure French movie he can find that's devoid of color filmmaking. The gentle-man pulls out a milk crate from beneath the counter. It's filled with battered and tattered DVD boxes, and a few VHS's here and there scattered in. He digs one out, showing me the front cover: *Une Nuit à Paris. One Night in Paris*, he says it's called. It's got an old black-and-white cover printed on it depicting a handsome man and a pretty lady embracing in the city streets illuminated by a single streetlamp. And it looks like it's raining, too. How ro-mantic. I know for a fact that Chloe hasn't seen this one because *I* haven't seen this one. The man tells me the price, five Euro, and he wraps the DVD up for me once I tell him it's a gift for a friend who's stuck studying a stack of books back in Berlin.

"Tell your friend to take a break sometime," the clerk tells me as he hands over my DVD wrapped in a brown paper envelope. "It's good for her. This movie will definitely help with that."

I thank the clerk kindly, in English and in French: "Thank you. *Merci.*"

And I'm back on the street, the Eiffel Tower now in sight as I continue East. It looms above me, spelling out wonder and prime tourism to any who bask in its glory. Even during the day it's beautiful, and I can't wait for the evening when I know it'll get lit up against the night skyline.

As I approach the tower with each step, I find that Paris can be as beautiful as it is lonely. I think to the wrapped-up DVD in my bag. *Une Nuit à Paris.* Oddly fitting, considering I have to pack up my things and leave tomorrow afternoon to board a plane back to Berlin.

So what does a girl like me get up to with only one night in Paris? For me, it's going to involve seeing the Eiffel Tower, stopping by the Louvre Museum, and then the Eiffel Tower again before I go to bed. Romantic, no, but exciting enough for me. And that's all that I need right about now.

I cross a bridge that passes over the river *Seine.* There are locks on this bridge, with initials etched onto each lock in permanent market, or carved in with sharp tools. I know couples come to Paris for the romance, and some put their initials on locks that have the key tossed into the river below, signifying the everlasting permanence of the romance as if it were locked down. As I pass over the bridge I peer at the locks clipped to the bridge's fence to see if I recognize any initials. M+R. A+C. DE+TS. EM+BO. No idea who any of these people are, but I'm sure they're happy. And I'm sure the love they had is permanent. At the very least, it's hard to forget someone when you spend time with them in the eternal city of love.

I finally cross over the bridge and make it to the park where the Eiffel Tower resides. I can't believe I'm really here, seeing the tower in person after only seeing it in photos for the entire two decades I've been alive. It's much more massive in person, I find that as you look up your neck feels like it's about to give way and you're going to fall back-end on your behind. I look around the park surrounding the tower. Couples sit on blankets, sharing bottles of wine and loaves of bread as they talk about this and that. Vendors carrying snacks, drinks and roses pass between those seated on the lawn, soliciting this and that as the couples wave them off or buy a rose or a snack for their significant other. A band plays off in the distance. I can see them close to the base of the tower. There's a Spanish guitar playing licks, a trumpet that toots the high notes, and a walking drum kit that keeps the tempo. They're playing a love song, I just know it.

I find a good spot and get myself set up as I empty a few contents from my backpack. I chug half a bottle of water I'd been hanging onto since I left the airport. Walking really does take it out of you.

I pull out my ukulele, too, and tune it up as I gaze up at the majesty of the tower. I strum out a few songs, ones I learned back home. "Somewhere Over the Rainbow," "I'm Yours," and "Master of Puppets" are just a few of my favorites that I know how to play well. Nobody around me pays any attention to my soft strumming. I try my best to keep time with the band playing just down the road, and the drum keeps me surprisingly on-tempo.

As I play the ukulele, I feel myself coming alive. It's like music awakens something in me. Before this semester abroad, I feel like I didn't have a passion in life. A North Star to guide me, you know? But now I know what it is: *music*. The ukulele opened a door for me, one that would hopefully guide me to a bright career in the industry, somewhere. I don't know what yet. All I know is that music is what I want to do when I go back home to Los Angeles to finish my studies. I plan on declaring a music major, at the very least. I haven't picked a major yet, so I'm in the prime of my studies, ready to follow my newfound dream.

A vendor passes by me, yanking me out of my deep thought as he offers me a pack of cigarettes. I decline, thanking him anyways. I go back to my uke a little more, eager to relax as I can pass the time sitting in front of humankind's greatest architectural prowesses. I decide I better check the time and pull out my phone. To my surprise I've been sitting here for over an hour, so I elect to pack up my things to head over to the Louvre museum.

Instead of walking to the museum, I take a cab. The driver knows what "Louvre" means well enough, and the meter on the tip of his dashboard tells me in plain English how many Euro I owe him once we reach our destination. I tip the driver ten percent, a normal flat rate for America. I don't know how tipping works over here in Europe, but the driver thanks me in French without giving me any of my change, so I figure tipping must be universal at this point.

I head inside the museum, where a strict and tired-looking woman about my age tells me that I can receive a student discount if I have valid ID. I pull it out, she gives me a discounted total, and before I know it I'm inside the grand halls of the Louvre. Arrows guide me through hallway after hallway, directing me toward the Mona Lisa herself.

As I gaze in the room housing the most famous portrait ever painted, I'm surprised at just how *small* the Mona Lisa really is. It's no larger than an eight by eleven sheet of printer paper, framed and hung up against a lonely wall. And the painting is surrounded by a horde of tourists holding up cameras and tablets and phones as they all try to take a picture of a painting they've seen printed a million times before. Nobody's here to soak up the moment. Every few minutes, a tourist tries to hop over the chain that keeps those from swarming the painting and attempts to take a selfie with the Mona Lisa; and every time I see that happen I also see a guard who escorts the attempted selfie-taker away from the room and out of the museum.

I take in the Mona Lisa for as long as I can until the tourists around me give me a headache. I slowly make my way out of the museum, passing by a few other well-known works that I've seen before. Eugene Delacroix's *Liberty Leading the People. Las Meninas* by Diego Velasquez. I've seen them in print before now, but never up-close in person. It really gives you perspective when you're seeing something so beautiful in person with your own eyes. I'm finding it hard to put the beauty into words. It's the same appeal to me as seeing your favorite artist live in concert, and I wish

Chloe was here to tell me all about her favorite live shows she's been to in college. She'd probably compare this visit here to a Kanye West concert: full of artistic energy and leaving you wanting more, more, more. I'm not that into Kanye, but I know what she means now as I pass through the museum, gazing on art that's influenced and defined human history for the past thousand-plus years.

I step outside the Louvre once I've seen my fill. I had no reason to stop by the gift shop this time around, and I check the time on my phone. 4:53pm. Enough time to make it back to the hostel to drop my bag off before I find dinner somewhere that's authentically Parisian. I elect to walk back to the hostel, taking the long way through the city as I think about where I'd like to eat for my one true dinner in Paris. I pass a wide street, the city buildings on either side plastered with illuminated posters and billboards that flash logos by on LCD screens. The Arc de Triomphe sits in the center of the square adjacent to all the billboards. I spot a few restaurants just down the street that look small and authentic enough, so I stop by one of them underneath their red-and-white striped awning to peer at a menu. Duck l'orange is on the menu, a French dish I've *always* wanted to try after reading about it in countless books and seeing it featured in countless movies. I jot down the name of the restaurant and the street on my phone, noting that dinner isn't served here until 8pm.

I continue the trek back to the hostel, and I reach the lobby close to 6:30pm. Still got some time to kill, I note, so I bid Clara a friendly hello from the front desk as I head back up to my room.

Someone else is here already, a boy my age unpacking a huge carry-on into the locker that rests beside mine. He's hunkered down, but I can still see how tall he is with a head of messy dark-brown hair. He's startled by my sudden entrance, and jumps up as I'm entering the room. His face is round and kind, dark eyebrows resting atop his brow. He's got smile lines, and I can just tell from the way he carries himself so aloof that he was probably a class clown back home.

And he's pretty cute to boot, too.

"Hey!" he practically yelps. I guess my sudden entrance startled him. "I'm Hunter. Guess I'm bunking below you?" he looks up at the bunk above him and sees a jacket I'd left behind.

"Guess so," I smile and climb up to the bed I'd put on reserve. I shut my eyes, in desperate need a break. I *really* want to look at Hunter, however, and when he asks me another question I have an excuse to open my eyes and gaze down at him, being careful not to stare.

"What's your name?"

"Annie Thompson," I reply.

"You visiting for the weekend, too, Annie?" he asks.

"Uh-huh."

"So, you leave tomorrow?"

"Yup."

"Me too," Hunter says. He sighs, and I feel his weight shift as he plops down on the bed below me. It shakes the bed frame just enough to keep me from falling asleep. I lean over the bed so I can keep looking at him while we talk.

He continues, "I don't know anybody here. I'm doing a work-study up north, staying with this family who took me in. They're going skiing in Switzerland this weekend, and I figured I'd take some time to come see what the big deal about Paris is for myself. What about you?"

I smile, careful not to stare at Hunter's bright green eyes I'm somehow just now noticing for the first time. "I'm studying abroad, too. Staying in Berlin with friends."

"How long have you been there?"

"Three months now. We leave in just around a month or so. Just need to get through finals."

"Man, that's lucky. Are your classes hard, then?"

I laugh. "Not in the slightest."

"What do you study?"

"In Berlin? General education things. But when I get back home, I want to study music."

Hunter looks around at the empty room we're in. "So...where *are* all your friends?"

"They're studying," I laugh again. "Back in Berlin, getting ready for finals. But they're evidently having a hard time getting the studying part of the study abroad down pat. So I'm here alone for the weekend. I don't mind, though."

Hunter nods. I can feel the bed frame rocking gently as he does so.

"Would you want to get a drink with me tonight, then?" he asks shyly.

Seems better than napping alone. And I'd like to get to know Hunter a little better, too. Already I find his presence warmingly infectious.

"Sure," I say. "But I'm going to get dinner at this place closer to eight. You're welcome to join me there, if you want. I thought I'd walk there, see the city as it lights up at night."

"That sounds amazing," Hunter says in a surprised tone. I bet he thought I'd say no. With a face like his, how could I ever decline? "I just can't believe I'm here, that's all. Paris is just so beautiful, don't you think?"

"Yeah," I smile. We pause for a few seconds, sitting comfortably in silence.

"Want to head out, then?" Hunter asks after a moment, and I find myself imbued with energy at his request. I spring up, hop down from the top bunk.

"Let's go," I say with a smile.

CHAPTER TWO

As Hunter and I walk through the streets of Paris in the cool, brisk evening, I find myself more and more interested in finding out just who he is back home. Hunter tells me this and that about his trip as we walk to the restaurant. He's a small-town boy back in Missouri, from a town of about two thousand people. By day, he goes to class at a college that's a forty-five minute drive from home, and he somehow finds time to work nearly forty hours a week at his local dollar store. This trip's a well-earned vacation, but he's still working to earn his keep. Hunter is staying in a village named *Fourcés,* up near the Pyrenees Mountains, where he's helping out a family with work not dissimilar to that of a maid. He doesn't care about the title, especially when he gets to stay in a nice villa overlooking the central square in town. He gets weekends off, and usually the family travels, leaving him alone for the better part of three days once a week.

Hunter's asking about me, too, and I find myself engrossed in our conversation. He's asking me questions that nobody's asked me in months. About my life back home in L.A., my friends, my family who I miss so dearly. It's really nice to have someone to talk to, and with each passing minute I find myself warming up even more to Hunter. He tells me about his life back home, and I listen carefully to find out just what kind of person I've partnered up with for the night.

"Back home, I'd probably just be playing video games right about now. Maybe drinking a beer or something, nothing fancy. Maybe playing games with the boys online over voice chat. I really don't know. What about you?"

"Well," I say, "I'd probably be reading a book or something. I like a quiet night in, nothing too crazy. Nights in L.A. can get kinda crazy out there, so when I stay home I can. I know, I'm boring."

"So you mean to tell me that you *don't* live an action-filled lifestyle filled with explosions and action stars? You could have had me fooled. You don't seem like the typical girl from Los Angeles, as far as I can tell."

"What do you mean by that?"

Hunter shrugs. "I mean, most girls I meet won't even give me the time of day. A guy like me from the midwest, asking out a Los Angeles girl like you? That would never happen back home."

"Well," I say with a sly smile. "We *aren't* back home though, are we?"

Hunter looks at me and smiles back. "We are not. That is correct. So, where's this place you were wanting to try again?"

"Just up ahead. I picked it out because it has duck l'orange. I hope that's okay with you."

"Oh, *hell yes it is!*" Hunter nearly jumps for joy, and I laugh at his antics. "I've *always* wanted to try duck l'orange. After seeing it in a thousand and one movies—"

"—you just need to try it for yourself!" I cut in, finishing his sentence. "Sorry, I'm exactly the same way."

Hunter smiles again, chuckles to himself. "Who would of thought two people like us would just...bump into to one another in a hostel, huh?"

I nod. "Small chance. And to think I thought you'd be a psycho murderer or something."

Hunter grins. "You don't know that for sure. Try me after a few beers, maybe I've recently escaped prison and you just don't know it yet."

I can't help but laugh at that, too. Hunter seems like the kind of person who couldn't hurt a fly even if he wanted. He tells me he's from Missouri. A good midwestern boy, I can tell. I can tell he's a softie underneath, but his edgy sense of humor keeps me on my toes well enough. I'm really starting to warm up to him, I find myself walking closer and closer to him as the sidewalk we're on gets more and more crowded. Our hands brush past one another's and I feel his soft and warm skin just for the briefest of moments. It's nice. It takes a lot of effort not to hang onto his hand for safe-keeping.

We pass a couple more blocks until we reach the restaurant I'd been wanting to visit, and Hunter holds the door open for me as we head inside.

A burly waiter with a pencil-thin black mustache directs us to a table for two. Hunter sits across from me, orders a glass of red wine for himself. I take a cup of coffee. I need to wake up if we're going to walk to the Eiffel Tower after this. Speaking of which—

"Any plans after this?" I ask Hunter casually. He shrugs.

"*None-zo.* Just meeting you has swept me off my feet, throwing all my caution and plans to the wind."

I giggle. "Well, I'm going to walk back over to the Eiffel Tower after eating if you want to join. I hear the lights are beautiful there this time of night."

Hunter nods. "I'm in."

Our waiter comes with our drinks and asks us if we're ready to order. Hunter nods, and we order our two plates of duck l'orange. The waiter stops us, his pencil-thin mustache quivering above his upper lip.

"Plates are very, *very* big," he says in a thick French accent. "Best to share if two."

I look at Hunter and he looks back at me. Our eyes hold the gaze for a second too long, and he blushes as I feel my face redden, too.

"One then, *s'il vous plaît,*" Hunter says. I fake surprise so I can tease him a little. But underneath, I'm very much impressed he speaks French. Very. Much. So.

"*Ooooh,* so you speak the local language, then?" I ask, grinning as my eyes widen with fake surprise. "Say something to me in French. I dare you."

Hunter chuckles, but obliges me anyways: "*Une jolie fille comme toi ne devrait pas passer une nuit aussi belle que ça seule,*" He says in a very dignified manner, waving his fork around like a conductor's baton as he speaks. I laugh. I ask him what he meant by that, but

Hunter just smiles and waves a hand away.

"I said this meal's going to be epic," Hunter blushes again. I know for a fact that *isn't* what he said, but I don't know enough French to call him out on it. He's really turning up the charm now, and I'm surprised as hell that an L.A. girl such as myself can be charmed by a midwestern boy like him. But he's doing it, alright.

The waiter brings us duck l'orange on a tray surrounded by freshly cooked asparagus, the orange citrus glaze on the duck glistening in the dim light of the restaurant. Two additional empty plates are brought out for us as well, and Hunter serves me a helping of duck first before helping himself.

"So, I see chivalry isn't dead just yet," I sarcastically swoon. Still, it's nice that he's thoughtful like that.

Hunter takes a sip of wine, staining his lips a full deep red that I can't help but stare at. Lips that...lips that might be nice to kiss. I find myself in utter shock at how fast I'd managed to fall for him, and I tell myself to keep playing it cool so he does't think I'm *too* desperate. I dive into my duck as well, and the taste is extraordinary. The citrus and vinegar sauce works *perfectly*, and the cooked skin of the duck comes apart easily, the meat melting in my mouth. It's the greatest thing I've ever tasted. It's like a billion tiny lights in my mouth, a party exclusively hosted for my taste buds. The saltiness of the duck and the orange citrusy-ness of the sauce pairs perfectly. It's a carefully-balanced taste that manages to improve with every bite. The duck meat's cooked perfectly, with the orange and salt bringing out even more flavor than I ever thought possible. I know coming here was well worth it. My dinner guest looks like he agrees, as he hasn't looked up from his plate since starting.

Hunter wipes his chin, offers me a napkin from the center of the table too. I blush again, wiping the sauce from my lips. I catch him glance down at my lips, too, and my heart skips a beat when I consider the notion that he's thinking the same kissing thoughts as me. Judging by the look on his face, I think he is.

"So, Annie," Hunter says, setting down his fork in between bites of delicious duck l'orange. "Do you...have someone back home, by chance? I just want to get to know you better. Any family you're missing? Friends you can't live without?"

I know he's probing to see if I've got a boyfriend back home. I decide to play along, just to see if I can get him to ask it explicitly.

"Back home? Well, there's a few people I miss. Friends, of course. Family, who doesn't miss them? But any boys back home? Well..."

Hunter pauses, takes another bite of duck as he ponders how to word his next phrase. "Anyone back home I should be afraid of, then?"

I giggle and shake my head. Hunter's kind of cute, and his act isn't subtle at all, making him that all the more charming. "No boyfriend back home, if that's what you're asking. Any boy I'd get close to back in the day would meet my friend Chloe and..." I trail off, worried I've said too much already. But Hunter's interested now.

"Oh? Who's Chloe?"

"An old friend of mine. We're actually roommates in Berlin, if I didn't mention her name before. But she's okay, I guess. She just jealous sometimes, that's all."

"Jealous of you?"

"And the guys I date. Or hook up with. More accurately, *try* to hook up with. Chloe gets one whiff of them and scares them off immediately. Jealously makes a person go crazy like that, but I know she does it out of love, you know?"

"Oh. Okay," Hunter says, and that's the end of that. I can see a hint of a smile he wears before taking the final bite of duck off his plate. I fiddle with the asparagus on the edge of my plate.

"What about you?" I ask, my turn to probe him. "Any pretty mademoiselles back home waiting for you?"

Hunter shakes his head. "Nobody, no. Nobody's waiting for Hunter Marshak for when he goes back home." He pauses, then adds, "Except for my mom. She's nice like that."

I fake a swoon. "Must be nice having a Ma to come home to."

"You don't?"

"I do but...it's complicated," I trail off. "My parents split up a few years ago while I was in high school, and my mom moved away. I haven't really seen her since the divorce. But it's okay, I guess. Her and Dad both paid for my trip out here. Mom hasn't really talked to me since I flew out to Berlin. I guess she's busy with her dating. Having an adult daughter around is just baggage that *no man* wants. At least, that's what she tells me all the time, *every time* we manage to find a time to talk."

Hunter shrugs, a look in his eyes says he's sympathetic toward my cause. "You mom doesn't know what she's missing out on," Hunter mutters, setting his fork and knife across his plate signifying to the waiter that he's finished. That's sweet of him to say.

I'm done with my plate, too, so I do the same as the waiter comes to collect our plates and drops off the check. Hunter dives for it, pulling out his wallet.

"I got this," he says in a very gentleman-like fashion. "You invited me out, so it's the least I can do."

I nearly blush, but wave his hands away from the bill as I snatch it up. "Trust me, I got this," I say. "Plus, like you said, *I'm* the one that invited you out. My treat."

Hunter smiles. "I got the next one, then." I'm not so sure we'll have time for a next one, but I nod anyways and smile as I pull out my traveller's credit card and hand it over to the waiter. "So, the Eiffel Tower, huh?"

I smile. "The Eiffel Tower. If you're up for it. If not, I can walk back to the hostel with you."

"Wow, what a charmer," Hunter says as he stands from the table. "So if *I* don't want to see the tower, you'll call it a night, too?"

I laugh. "No, I said I'd walk you back to the hostel. I didn't say anything about staying there."

Hunter laughs, too. "Good thing I'm down to see the tower, then. Plus, I hear the view is spectacular at night."

"Let's go, then," I say, standing up as I reach for my jacket. "We've got a walk ahead of us with plenty of opportunities to rest along the way."

And just like that, we're out the door and on the way to the grand Eiffel Tower, just a handful of blocks to the East.

CHAPTER THREE

As Hunter and I walk down the bustling Parisian street at night, we find ourselves strolling closer to one another than ever before. Hunter asks me about my hobbies and what I like to do for fun back home, and part of me wants to freak out. I'm worried that I'm boring him with my life story, but he listens intently as I prattle on.

"Well, I've always managed to find time for a good book," I explain. "That, or an old movie. My roommate and I, Chloe, love watching them. Especially the romantic ones. We just *love* those."

"Any good recommendations I should check out, then?"

"Well, not necessarily a recommendation, but I *did* pick something up on the way to the tower on my first walk-through. It's in my bag back at the hostel. I'll show it to you when we get back."

"I've got my laptop back at the hostel, too," Hunter says slyly. "We can always give it a watch, just to make sure it's safe for your roommate to watch, too."

I laugh. "Maybe we can," I quip back. "You never know."

We continue our walk down the Rue to the bridge just between our hostel and the Eiffel Tower. The tower's just up ahead, but the lights have yet to come on. As Hunter and I pass by the locks clamped to the bridge's fence, the tower lights up, winking on suddenly and nearly blinding onlookers around us. Hunter and I both gasp in awe, and we look at one another with unfettered delight as we continue our walk to the park, just below the tower.

The air around us cools as the evening stretches on. Hunter's hand brushes against mine again as we cross the street just past the bridge that's now behind us. We make our way over to the *Champ de Mars*, the field in front of the Eiffel Tower, and I'm shocked to see groups of people that were here during my first visit. The band's still under the tower, still jamming away. I see a few couples, still sprawled out on their same blankets and all. I admire the dedication. I couldn't sit still for that long, and I secretly admire their ability to find such inner peace.

"Look," I point, directing Hunter's view to the base of the tower. "That band's been here *all day*, they were playing when I was here this afternoon. And that couple, passed out on the blanket? They shared a picnic this afternoon. I guess the wine must've got to them."

The band playing just under the base of the tower plays a slower song than before, something a little more romantic. I've heard the melody a thousand times before but can't put my finger on the melody. Suddenly, Hunter chimes in, pointing at the band as we continue to walk around the park.

"They're playing that Dean Martin song, *That's Amore*," he says matter-of-factly. "I hear it all the time back home. The band at our prom played it, too, only it wasn't nearly as good as this version."

"Aww, you went to prom?" I tease Hunter, gently poking at his side. "How was it? Did you have a cute date?"

Hunter laughs and shakes his head. "Me and the boys went stag, you know? Going solo."

I chuckle. "Meet anyone special there? Anyone *I* should be worried about?"

Hunter shakes his head again. "Stuck out that night. I had a girl that I *was* dancing with, if you must know."

"Oh?"

"Her name was Jenna McDougal. Jenna had a snaggletooth. Anyways, we had chemistry class together, and the chemistry was still…still kinda there that night. But she didn't like my jokes, so halfway through the last slow dance she ditches me and leaves with her friends. Not like I cared too much, anyways. My friends and I got pancakes after the prom anyways, which I'm *sure* Jenna would have made all about herself and her god damn snaggletooth. So I think *I'm* the lucky one, really. Did you go to your prom?"

I shake my head. "Didn't go. Too much trouble." I keep walking, but Hunter stops dead in his tracks.

"You didn't go?" he asks with genuine surprise. "I figured a girl like you would end up prom queen. You're serious?"

I nod. "Deadly serious."

"Too many good books and movies back home, then?" Hunter's still standing still as he interrogates me, looking around at the park surrounding us.

"Yeah," I say. "Too much fun at home."

Then Hunter holds out a hand to me, and I wonder if it's in jest or not. But he's not laughing or smiling, so I guess he's serious.

"May I have this dance, then?"

I blush, hard this time. Hunter keeps looking at me expectantly, his hand still outstretched. *What the hell,* I think to myself as I take his hand. Hunter grips my hand in his and brings me in close as his other hand grips my waist tight. He rocks back and forth to the beat of the band playing *That's Amore* behind us. We sway to the music, an impromptu prom of our own as we're surrounded by total strangers and the light from the Eiffel Tower illuminates our steps.

We dance together for a few minutes without speaking a word. Hunter pulls me in even closer, and I turn my head to rest my chin against his shoulder. It's really nice, dancing like this. Even nicer are how warm Hunter's hands are, the rough callouses telling me he knows how to work with his hands. How I can gently feel his ribs pressed up against my chest. He's taller than me by a good six inches, at least, and for just the briefest of moments I'm whisked away to a whole other world full of romance and passion and love. It's almost too much, and I look up at Hunter who's already gazing down at me.

Before we can say anything, however, I feel a presence behind me and I step back away from Hunter. It's a vendor, carrying a sack full of glass bottles that hangs in a pouch around his neck with a bouquet of roses in his free hand. The vendor's a short guy, shorter than me with a buzz cut and a strong odor of cigarettes.

"Champagne for the lady?" he asks Hunter, but Hunter laughs

and shakes his head.

"Not tonight, thanks."

"A rose, then."

The vendor hands a rose over to Hunter who accepts it without realizing the vendor's holding out his other hand for payment. Hunter shrugs, hands the vendor a Euro coin before he's off to the next spot to harass someone else, leaving us alone in a half-dance, half-embrace as Hunter looks at the rose with confusion.

"I guess this is for you," Hunter says, handing me the rose. I blush again. It's almost too much for me. Fortunately, it's dark enough to where Hunter can't see my reddening cheeks, but I can't tell if he's blushing the same way, either.

I take the rose and clamp it between my teeth like a Spanish flamenco dancer, and Hunter laughs.

"I didn't take you for the type who knows how to tango," he says jokingly. "I'm a little rusty, but I can follow along."

I laugh. "No need. Let's find a place to sit down anyways. I'm exhausted after that dance," I say with a wink. "I'll need to get my energy back if we're going to make it back to the hostel in one piece."

Hunter nods, and we scour the park for any bench or slab of concrete we can sit down at as we walk another lap around the green. But then I spot a museum, across from the tower in an adjacent park, and. I suggest we head that way to sit down. Hunter agrees.

Along the way, my phone buzzes loudly in my pocket.

"Whoah," Hunter says. "Deaf much?"

"Sorry," I giggle, pulling it out to check my notifications. "It's on silent. It just buzzes loud, I guess."

I've got one new text message. From Chloe. It's a selfie of her and Daisy out at a club. "STUDYING HARD!" she writes. I sigh. Of course the study session didn't last long.

I put my phone away, giving all my attention to Hunter as we continue to make our way over to the museum. Along the way we're harassed by street vendor after street vendor.

"Champagne for the *mademoiselle*?"

"A rose for the lady?"

"Memorabilia and buttons, sir, if you would wish to purchase or browse."

Hunter shakes all the vendors off with a casual wave of his hand, protecting me from the endless solicitation of Parisian merchants looking to make a quick buck from a pair of lonely tourists.

We make our way over to the museum finally, where I can see posters adoring the columns, advertising a new gallery and exhibit that just opened this past week about some Egyptian prince or king or whatever. Rameses II was an endlessly fascinating pharaoh, Hunter tells me as we sit down and gaze upon the Eiffel Tower in all its glory. We sit down on the steps of the museum, facing the tower in all its glory as I rest my aching dogs. Hunter's massaging his foot, too, and he tells me all he knows about Ramses II while we rest.

"I don't know. He just…knew how to build amazing monuments, I guess. That's a skill the old Egyptians had. Building things. Something like that is a talent that shouldn't ever be put to waste."

"Didn't the ancient Egyptians use slaves, though?" I ask earnestly. Hunter nods.

"A shame they did. And when people claim the pyramids were built by aliens, it devalues the hard work of the million nameless slaves that did all the heavy lifting."

I gasp and feign surprise. "You mean the pyramids *weren't* built by extraterrestrials flying around in UFO's? Well, you certainly could have fooled me."

"But think about it. We're gazing at the Eiffel Tower, which was *not* built by slaves. And they don't charge us a thing to gaze upon its beauty. We just have to remember the builders ourselves when it comes to things like this. I don't know. Just something to think about, I guess."

I nod, and Hunter and I sit in perfect silence for a while as the Eiffel Tower's lights flash on and off, resulting in an endless pattern of beauty that you can't really imagine until you see it for yourself. The tower lights up, brighter than the city around us, and all you can do is stop and stare when it's alight. The twinkling patterns keep you watching, and the illuminated construction beams give you all the more appreciation for the achievements in architecture. I couldn't imagine a more beautiful sight lighting up the world around me.

Another vendor approaches us, and this time we watch him as he climbs the steps toward us, carrying a usual sack of glass bottles and bouquet of roses.

"Champagne for the lady?" he asks us, and Hunter nods this time.

"How much for a bottle?"

"Ten Euro."

"I'll give you fifteen for two bottles," Hunter proposes. The vendor nods in agreement, and the two make the exchange quickly before the merchant is off, hunting his next target.

Hunter's holding two bottles of champagne. I tuck the rose behind my ear, careful to make sure the thorns have all been clipped before I make a fool of myself.

"Know how to open these?" Hunter asks playfully. I shake my head.

"I'll just get champagne everywhere," I say. "You open them up."

Hunter laughs as he stands up, a bottle in each hand. "You just watch and learn," he says. I see his thumbs rise up the bottles's necks as he twists off the metal wires holding the corks in place. Suddenly, both bottles erupt with a massive *POP!* and Hunter's holding two fountains of champagne that burst out into the world. Around us, a few passerby clap as Hunter takes a grandiose bow.

"Thank you, thank you."

He sits back down once the foam's all been spat out from the bottle, handing me a bottle of champagne. I nod and take a sip. It's cheap, but does the job. The bubbles warm my throat and tickle my tongue as the sweet nectar slides down my throat. Hunter takes a chug from his bottle and wipes his mouth. We drink our champagne out of the bottles, looking on as the Eiffel Tower lights its lights up again in the beautiful twinkling pattern I'd come to expect.

For just a moment, we stop and look into one another's eyes. I can just make out the bright green of his irises. He smiles, and looks back to the tower, taking another drink of his champagne.

It's all just too perfect, really.

CHAPTER FOUR

After a little while longer of taking in the sights, Hunter and I stand up and stumble as we sway to try and catch our footing. I'm definitely tipsy, to say the least. The champagne bottles are all empty now, and I feel drunker than I usually do when I drink champagne. I guess the Parisian nectar does wonders for tourists, but I also think the fact that I've had an entire bottle to myself probably explains the drunkness well enough. Hunter's having a hard time walking, too, and we laugh as our arms inexplicably link up as we start the trek back to the hostel.

It's a perfect night—one that I wish would never end.

Our elbows are interlocked, and I can feel his skin flush from drunkness. Or he's embarrassed. Or he likes me as much as I'm liking him. I hope for the third option, but I'm ready to accept the first two as perfectly valid reasons as well. He's looking straight ahead, an odd sense of determination that peeks through his intoxication. He's utterly charming, and I giggle as I look at the serious mug of a man that I've only known for half a day.

"So, what now?" I slur. Hunter laughs.

"I think we better get back to the hostel in one piece," he says. "Don't worry. I'll escort you there. You're safe with me," and he puffs up his chest comically as I double over in laughter.

"I'm sorry, I'm sorry. I'm not laughing at your chest, I promise," I wave my hands in a feeble attempt to reassure him. "It's just —it's just…oh, I'm *so* drunk!"

Hunter laughs. "Me too. Come on, it's only a few more blocks. I think."

We pass by the restaurant from before. The LCD billboards lined up and down the block are as bright as ever, perhaps even brighter than the Eiffel Tower itself. We pass by the Arc de Triomphe and Hunter grabs my arm and jerks me to one side to avoid an oncoming car.

The car swerves past us, the driver honking with French anger at the American tourists making a mockery of his city in our drunken stupor. I can't blame him for being mad, honestly. *At least Hunter's got me*, I think to myself as I hang on for dear life.

"Careful!" he says, gripping my arm tighter than usual. I feel protected. Safe. Already I know I'm going to miss Hunter once I have to fly back to Berlin. I wonder if he's going to miss me just as much. As Hunter holds my arm, still tight as ever, I look up into his gorgeously green eyes. He's gazing down at me again, smiling.

I think he's going to miss me, too.

We continue our walk back to the hostel, where we are let back in by Clara the receptionist.

"Clara, how many hours do you work a day?" I ask her, careful not to slur my words too much. She can probably tell I'm drunk, but obliges me nevertheless.

"I work twelve-hour shift," Clara says. "I like it."

I shrug, turning around. Hunter's already bounding up the stairs two at a time like an animal, and I laugh as I hurry to catch up with him.

Back in our room, we see that no other guests have checked into our room. I look at the clock on my phone. 11:38pm. Check-in ended a little over half an hour ago, so we now know for sure that the room is all ours for the evening.

Hunter plops on his bed face-down. I scramble up to the top bunk, but not before grabbing my backpack out of my locked cabinet down below. I drunkenly yank the backpack open and pull out the brown paper-wrapped bag that housed the DVD I bought for Chloe, *One Night in Paris.*

"Wanna watch?" I dangle the DVD down below the bed for Hunter to see. I hang over the side of the bed to gauge his reaction, but he's still laying there, motionless.

"Hmmmm," he mutters, his face still pressed against the covers and pillows on his bed. He's probably not getting up anytime soon.

"Make room, then," I say playfully. "Where's your laptop at?"

"B-*bag*," he mutters drunkenly, and points to his locked cabinet adjacent to mine. He pulls a key out of his pocket and hands it over to me and I unlock his locker, pulling out his ratty backpack he'd been traveling with. One of the straps is ripped clean off, and two of the three zippers are utterly and hopelessly jammed beyond belief. I open the top pouch, the only one with a working zipper, and pull out Hunter's laptop. There are stickers adorning the laptop's shell. Stickers that are in the shape of all the continents of the world. Some band stickers I don't recognize, and some other cool designs that may or may not have come from skateboarding shops. I only recognize those because of the million and one skate shops that litter LA. I unwrap the DVD, insert it into the laptop's disc drive, and the main menu starts up.

Hunter sits up and leans against the wall adjacent to the bed. I scootch back, leaning up next to him as close as I can without coming on too strong. I don't want to make him nervous or anything, but I find subtlety is much more difficult when you've just about downed an entire bottle of champagne in one sitting.

"Whazzat again?" Hunter asks through tired eyes.

"*Une Nuit à Paris,* I think it means something like a world full of Paris, or something like that. I forget. The guy who sold it to me said it was good, though."

"*One Night in Paris,*" Hunter mutters.

"Huh?"

"That's—*hic*—that's the title. *One Night in Paris.* And the guy that sold this to you is right. I've seen this one before, I think."

Huh. Hunter continues to impress me with every sentence he utters. I would never have taken him for a French cinephile. But hey, life can always surprise you like that, right?

"You know I speak French, right?" Hunter giggles.

"Yeah?" I play along. "Say something in French."

"*Une jolie fille comme toi ne devrait pas passer une nuit aussi belle que ça seule,*" he says carefully and slowly, pronouncing everything perfectly. As far as I can tell, I mean. I don't speak French.

"What's that mean?"

"A pretty girl like you shouldn't spend a beautiful night like this alone."

I blush. He's too charming. And I'm too drunk. I should have kissed him under the Eiffel Tower. I *should* kiss him now, but some part of me wants to hold off. So I do. I start the movie up. It's a cute oldie, alright. There's a guy alone in Paris, walking the streets when he meets a beautiful dame sitting alone in a restaurant. The movie's so old the dialogue is spelled out in title cards between shots. Poorly translated, I may add. Anyways, the man sees the dame and goes inside the restaurant and orders an espresso— which the translators misspelled as "EXPRESSO" when doing the subtitling cards, but I digress. Hunter manages to stay awake, but I can feel him drifting off to sleep every once in a while. His head leans over against my shoulder and I don't brush it off.

The movie keeps going. The man and the dame meet and hit it off. They go for a stroll around town, and the black-and-white film reel captures the city skyline perfectly in every shot. The two walk hand-in-hand, and it's revealed that they actually once knew each other. They embrace in the long lost memories of yesterday and of love that's been lost once before. I wonder if Hunter and I will ever meet up again like that. I can't really imagine us doing so, but a girl can dream, can't she?

The movie wraps up, and I'm surprised at just how short it is. Barely an hour long. I shut the laptop and look over at Hunter, who's on the verge of passing out. He looks at me and winks. I laugh.

"Not yet," I slur, and I instantly regret saying that. A simple *'no'* would have worked, but now I've gone and blown my cover. I'm sure he won't care. It's not like we're going to see each other after tomorrow, anyways, so what does it matter?

I stumble back up to my bed after locking Hunter's laptop away safely in the cabinet. We say an awkward goodnight, and I pass out almost instantly. Sleep washes over me, and I don't dream about anything. Real life has become the dream for me.

CHAPTER FIVE

I wake up the next morning with the worse hangover I've ever had the misfortune of experiencing. My head is *killing me.* I remember only a foggy haze, but the recollection comes back to me as I wonder why the hell I'd ever down an entire bottle of champagne on my own. Then I remember.

Hunter. I met Hunter yesterday, and we hit it off. We shared dinner and a slow dance under the Eiffel Tower.

And we didn't kiss.

I peer over the side of the hostel bunk bed to see if he's still passed out, but to my dismay the bed is completely empty and made up already. He's nowhere to be seen.

A pit sinks in my stomach, and I feel a horrid sense of dread. Had Hunter already left for the day? Did he have trouble remembering last night, too? Did he forget about me? I hope he didn't, but with each passing moment as I stare at his empty bed I find the dark reality setting in that he may have disappeared from my life entirely, as quickly as he entered it last night.

We didn't even get to say goodbye.

I get up, pick out a change of clothes from my locker and head into the shared bathroom to shower off my hangover. I take a hot shower, the steam fogging up the mirror as I brush my teeth, silently praying that Hunter hadn't really left town yet. After I finish up in the bathroom, I lock my stuff away in the locker and head downstairs to the lobby for the complimentary breakfast that's served in the hostel every morning according to the advertisement I read online.

And that's where Hunter is.

He's sitting at a large table, a plate of bread, ham and cheese in front of him as he sips an espresso and reads something on his phone. As I make my way down the stairs and into view, Hunter looks up at me and beams. He remembers everything, thank God.

I take a seat across from him and smile. "Thought you'd packed up and left without me," I say casually. Hunter shakes his head.

"Wouldn't have done so without saying goodbye first. You got a flight to catch today?"

I nod. "Unfortunately. It leaves in, like, six hours."

"Me, too. Mine's a little later. We still have plenty of time," Hunter says. "Clara was just telling me about this café uptown where they have *cats* running around! Cats!"

"A cat café?" I ask. That sounds intriguing. I look over to the receptionist desk, where Clara stands. She smiles at me and I wave back. Fortunately for Hunter, I *love* cats. I've got one back home I miss dearly. A big, fat, orange tabby cat who's living with my Dad. Mister Fluffypants is his name, but he goes by Pants for short.

Hunter shows me on a map where the cat café is. It's a ten minute walk from here, so I stock up on breakfast and eat as we discuss what we can fit in our schedules today.

"Cat café, then lunch?" Hunter asks. "I can call you a cab, too. Make sure you get back to the airport in one piece."

"I would *so* appreciate that," I say in earnest. "The metro's a little scary for someone who doesn't read French. I'd hate to get lost when I've got a flight to catch."

Hunter smiles. "It's a date, then."

We stroll up to the cat café, taking our sweet time to soak in the early Paris morning. The air doesn't reek too strongly of cigarettes today, for which I'm ever thankful.

Hunter takes my hand in his. We're awake, sober, full of coffee. This isn't a mistake at all. It's purely intentional, and I grip his hand tight as we cross street after street on our way to the café. It's a perfect day outside, as the sun peeks out from between white fluffy clouds above. We see the cat café just up ahead, a large circular sign with a pretty black kitty cat hanging above a glass-paned door just below a red awning. The café has some French name I can't read, and Hunter tells me it loosely translates to 'cat café' anyways, so I don't worry about getting the name wrong in my head.

Inside, the café's a small-ish establishment, with only a few scattered tables here and there for the patrons to sit after making their order up at the front counter.

On the other hand, the lack of tables are made up for the amount of cats that sit in every corner of the room, mewing to themselves as they chatter and patter around the restaurant floor. Inside, there are old-fashioned pinup posters hanging from the wall. Old war propaganda. Looks like there's some postcards in a collage just behind the front counter. Through the old-fashioned bubbly windows, we can see the horde of cats. Hunter and I step inside gingerly, careful to make sure that none of the kitties escape and run out into the street. A lone employee behind the counter greets us, a plump old woman with jet-black hair tied up into a bun with an infectious smile on her face. She introduces herself as Maggie, the owner, and she wipes her hands on her apron that hangs from her neck and extends a hand for Hunter and I to shake before we order our espressos.

Maggie brings the espressos out to us as Hunter and I pick a table. One table has a cat sitting atop it, a tiny orange-and-white mix who mews politely at Hunter as he sits down. Hunter coos, petting the kitty cat and I can't help but feel as warm and fuzzy inside as the kitty he's petting. I sip my espresso, peering over the rim at Hunter as he drinks his too. We don't have to say anything to feel comfortable with just one another's company. It took me and Chloe *years* to get to this point.

"So," Hunter says after setting his cup down, careful to keep it out of the way of his new orange-and-white friend. "You're going back to Berlin."

"Yup," I say, nodding glumly. "Back to Berlin."

"Shame. We just started getting to know each other, too."

I know where he's going with this, and part of me wants to jump for joy. The rest of me manages to keep the excitement stifled down, knowing full well that if I look too eager he may reconsider the offer I know he's about to propose.

"Yeah, how about that?" I ask with purpose. "Shame you're not going to be in Germany anytime soon. Or else I'd ask you to come help me study for finals. I'm pretty stressed over a math final, but that's about it."

"I'm terrible at math," Hunter says in earnest. "But I'd..." He trails off, and I cock my head to one side. Hunter's kitty friend, still sitting atop our table, cocks his head too, and Hunter continues after a brief pause:

"I'd love to come visit you sometimes, I mean. If you're okay with it."

I smile. "I'd really like that."

Hunter smiles too. "Then we might as well exchange numbers. To get in touch, you know?"

I pull out my phone and Hunter punches his number in for me. "There. Now you can text me whenever. Just to give you an easy out in case you actually *don't* want to call that creepy guy you met in Paris that one night."

I laugh. "This has all been one great acting gig. I'm getting paid a boatload by some Hollywood exec just to lead you on. But I'm glad you're able to pick up on it. Because *now* that means I'm free from their servitude."

Hunter adds: "Now, if you'll just give me your *real* name instead of your stage name, I'll be all set—" and we both double over in laughter as the orange-and-white kitty between us hops down from the table, startled by the sudden outburst.

We finish our espresso and leave Maggie a good tip between the two of us. As we head out of the cat café and back into the Parisian cityscape, Hunter checks his phone.

"Don't you have to get ready for your flight soon?"

"Don't remind me," I say. "We should make one more stop before heading back to the hostel. What do you think?"

"I think that's stupendous," Hunter says. "What did you have in mind?"

I take Hunter to the old movie store I'd gone to yesterday. The same old clerk is still manning the front counter and recognizes me when I bring Hunter in.

"Ahh, *Une Nuit à Paris* returns again. Tell me, did you give your friend the gift yet?"

I shake my head. "No, but we watched it last night."

"And tell me, what did you think of it?"

I beamed. "It was swell. Really swell. Got anything else for us to check out? We've got time for one more stop here, and I wanted to get another souvenir."

Hunter peruses the stacks of movies as the clerk goes back for the milk crate of old forgotten classics. I browse through the crate, but nothing jumps out at me. *One Night in Paris* jumped out at me when the clerk brought it out before, but now as I scour the old bin for something to watch back home, I can't find anything. Nothing's as unique or original as *One Night in Paris,* however. It's as if that single movie ruined all old movies for me. I can't get over it. I look over to Hunter, who's curiously eyeing an old Russian import monster movie.

"Find anything?" I holler over. He shakes his head.

"Not unless you count big beefy boys named Boris dressed up in rubber suits destroying miniature cities. No."

I laugh, shake my head. "Come here and help me find something, then."

Hunter comes over and starts digging through the milk crate of classics with me. We see old war movies, a cowboy movie that was *clearly* filmed in Italy, a collection of animated shorts produced by an old French company. Nothing stands out. Hunter shrugs.

"Sometimes you find a gem. I guess *Une Nuit à Paris* was that for you."

"So all other movies are ruined for me now?"

"I wouldn't say that," Hunter counters. "I'd say it was one of the most memorable experiences of your life. But life goes on. New movies always come out. Old ones get rediscovered. And you'll always have *One Night in Paris* when you go back home."

Hunter was totally right, but my heart still ached.

Then, I realize. I'm not upset because the movie *One Night in Paris* was great, I'm upset because I know I probably won't see Hunter ever again. Sure, we'll make plans to meet up here or there, but life happens. Plans fall through. Life goes on as the new movies keep coming out and coming out.

I can't find the words to tell Hunter how I feel. We thank the clerk for letting us browse around and head back outside.

"Back to the hostel?" I ask Hunter. He nods.

"Back to the hostel," he says glumly. I can tell he's upset our time is coming to an end, too. As we walk back, our hands don't brush. Our arms don't link, and Hunter doesn't hold me tight as cars swerve close past us on the crowded city streets.

We make it back to the hostel in record time. I pack my things quickly, as I didn't bring that many belongings with me to begin with. I re-cover and seal up the copy of *Une Nuit à Paris* for Chloe when I get back to Berlin. Hunter sees my ukulele and his eyes widen.

"Hey, you play?" he nods at my uke case, and I smile.

"Yeah, I do. What about you?" Hunter shakes his head.

"I played drums when I was younger, but nothing new anymore. You know how it gets in life, sometimes, when you're super busy and you can't work on any hobbies like you used to? Yeah, that happened to me."

I pull out the ukulele, making sure the four strings are all in tune before giving it a hearty strum.

"I think we've got time for a song together, if you'd like to sing something with me."

Hunter grins. "You wouldn't happen to know *Master of Puppets*, do you?"

I laugh harder than I'd ever laughed before. Because of course I know *Master of Puppets*.

"Follow my lead, I'll cue you in."

◆　◆　◆

We play a song together, laughing all the while as Hunter belts out the chorus to the Metallica classic. I strum as quickly as I can, keeping the song in tempo as Hunter and I share one last moment together before I'm gone for good.

Afterwards, we finish packing and Hunter escorts me out of the hostel after I check out with Clara. Clara bids me *adieu*, wishing me farewell on my next journey. I can't explain why, but I almost tear up saying goodbye to the receptionist who made my life easier this past day. I get so emotional I nearly hug Clara, but we say goodbye nevertheless as Hunter and I head out into the street to hail a cab.

We have to walk for a few blocks before we see any taxis, but Hunter manages to wave one down for me.

"You riding along?" I ask Hunter from the cab window once I've loaded my stuff in. "It'd make the long ride back to the airport easier."

Hunter shakes his head. "I've got a few more places I'd like to see. Besides, I've got a late night flight anyways. Hey, I'll see you in Berlin, right? You'll just have to text me first since I don't have your number."

I smile the sweetest smile I can muster. "I'll text you for sure. Just don't be a stranger, okay?"

"Okay," Hunter smiles, and just like that the cab's rolling away from the curb. I turn around, waving goodbye to Hunter through the rear window. The cab pulls through a one-way street and then out into a roundabout, joining the rest of the Parisian day traffic.

"Shoulda kissed him," the cabbie mutters with a thick accent from the driver's seat. "Way you two were talking, you should have kissed him."

I sigh, lean back into my seat. "You're probably right," I agree. "Just get me to the airport."

"*Oui*," the cabbie mutters, and we're on the road without any further discussion.

CHAPTER SIX

Arriving back in Berlin I find Chloe, Daisy and Samantha all waiting for me at the Berlin Tegel Airport. They're just outside receiving, holding up a comically large sign with "ANNIE" written on it in large permanent marker. As I walk over to them with a friendly wave, we all break down in giggles and embrace.

"How was studying?" I ask. Daisy shrugs, and Samantha waves her hand dismissively.

"We're fine," she says. "Don't worry about our stupid test scores. Tell us, *how was Paris?*"

Now it's my turn to shrug. "Okay, I guess."

"Okay, *you guess?*" Chloe scoffs. "Okay, you were *definitely* up to something then. Spill the beans, Annie."

I both do and don't want to tell them about Hunter. For one, they're all going to want to meet him when he comes and visits Berlin. Second, I know Chloe gets jealous easily. She's going to try to grill him to see if he's scared off easily. I know this because Chloe *always* does this when I bring a guy around, whether it was back in high school or just a casual fling in Berlin before I met Hunter. She'd always find a way under his skin, asking just the right questions to get him to leave and never call me again. One time, the guy ended up calling *Chloe* back, which really stung.

So I'm not telling them about Hunter.

I shrug my shoulders. "I saw the Eiffel Tower. The Louvre. Had duck l'orange. Oh, and I even went to a café where there are cats *everywhere*. Plus, I got us all a movie we can watch later. Check it out."

Standing in the airport receiving bay, I rifle through my backpack and pull out the brown-paper wrapped gift for Chloe and hand it over to her. She tears through the paper gleefully and gasps when she sees the cover to *Une Nuit à Paris.*

"It's perfect!" Chloe says, smiling through gritted teeth. She's weirdly put off by the gift, I can tell. I don't know why, and before I have a chance to think about it any further she pulls me in for a hug. "Thank you so much!"

But I still feel that pang of doubt. That doubt starts to trickle into the forefront of my mind, and I worry whether or not Chloe really likes the gift or not. She loves old movies, just like me, but she doesn't have the connection to the DVD like I do. No memories watching it with Hunter like I do. I feel worried, but I shove it aside as Daisy and Samantha say we need to get back to the apartment soon. Chloe puts the DVD in her overstuffed purse, agreeing with our friends. They're all hungry, turns out. I'm famished, too, and we all agree to head back and split a cab four ways.

We arrive back at the apartment pretty late after stuffing our faces with top of the line bratwurst from a highly-rated restaurant just downtown. Samantha and Daisy are pooped, and the two of them are off to bed as soon as we're back. Chloe and I decide to stay up a little bit, and we pop into the living room to watch the DVD I had brought back. At least with Daisy and Samantha going to bed I know Chloe won't gossip with them about me tonight. At least, I *hope.* Chloe's a notorious gossip, and Daisy and Sam are usually pulled into whatever she's got going on at the moment. I worry it'll be me soon that takes the brunt of the gossip.

Before pressing play, Chloe looks over at me suspiciously.

"There's something you're not telling me about your trip," she says. I cock my eyebrows at her, calling her bluff.

"Such as?"

"You met someone. I can just smell it on you. Look at you, you're totally guilty. Spill the beans," Chloe says for the second time today, this time sterner than before. I can tell I'm getting to her. I'm the one that's getting under her skin for once.

"Chloe, I'm being totally honest with you. *I didn't meet anyone in Paris.*"

She sighs, shrugs. "Whatever. Suit yourself," as she passively aggressively presses play.

Watching *Une Nuit à Paris* with Hunter was a dream I never thought I'd have come true. Watching that same movie with Chloe, however, is a stark contrast. She constantly pauses the movie to ask me about Paris, asking me two more times if I'd *really* met anyone there. She texts throughout and even gets up to take a phone call without at least pausing it or asking me first. Then, of course, she comes back into the room and asks what she missed. I catch her up to speed, but Chloe's back on her phone by the time I'm finished talking. And then I realize she's been doing this all semester. Conversations are constantly interrupted by her need to make a phone call. She's never paying attention, and I always find myself re-explaining things because she couldn't be bothered to look away from her phone for ten seconds.

When the movie's over I breathe a silent sigh of relief and head back to my room. Chloe hangs out in the common area, still texting whoever it is she's always texting. I shut the door to my bedroom, closing me off to the world around me. My room here in Berlin isn't much, but it's home. I have a few pictures of my friends from back home hanging up around my bed, a few old photos of my parents mixed in there, too. I place my ukulele back on the stand sitting on the corner and open the double window to let the bright Berliner sunlight into my room. It's mid-afternoon, and all my classes for tomorrow wound up getting cancelled this morning. Fortunately I don't ever have that much homework.

I pull out my phone and sit on my bed. I send a text to Hunter's number saved in my phone.

"Hey :) it's that girl you met in Paris. What's up?"

My phone buzzes a second after I press send.

"Hey, it's that psycho killer clown from Paris. I've got an open weekend in two weeks, thinking about heading to Berlin to meet up with some random crazy chick I met in a hostel in Paris just the other day. She's awesome. I can't wait to see her. I can come see you too, if you

like. ;) Drop me a line if mid-December works for you."

I laugh out loud. I can't believe how much better my day is already just hearing from him.

I type out a response.

"Tell that chick I said hello, and then come see me if she doesn't kill you first. Mid-December works fine for me. Hope to hear from you again."

I send the text, and not even ten seconds later my phone buzzes.

"Hey, it's Hunter, hope your hearing still works. Your phone buzzes louder than anyone's I've ever met. You should get that checked out. I can always text you again if you need to run another hearing test, just in case you're worried about going deaf or anything."

He's just too perfect. I clutch my phone tight to my chest and lay back on my bed, looking up at the ceiling. I can't believe this. It's like I'm floating on air.

My phone buzzes again.

"Can't wait to see you in a few weeks. P.S.: there is no other girl from Paris, in case you were wondering."

I wasn't, but it feels good to hear him say that.

CHAPTER SEVEN

Just before mid-December finally rolls around, Hunter and I text one another back and forth constantly. A simple *'hey ;)'* between classes here, a long *'I can't wait to show you around Berlin when you fly in'* there. It keeps me going for those few weeks while Chloe and I verbally spar every day.

Things with her have been heating up. She's been growing jealous of me, I can tell. Of *me*. Chloe, who's always on her phone texting whomever, found herself getting enraged with jealousy once I finally pried myself away from her for more than a few minutes every day. She can't stand the notion of me finding someone who wants to be around me as much as I want to be around them. With Chloe, she always has something else going on before me. She keeps me on reserve, whenever we make plans she's usually texting me: *'just in case something else doesn't come up later,'* letting me know full well that I was her backup for the night.

And now, she's furious. I can hear her stomping around the apartment when she knows we're both home. I doubt she does it when I'm gone. She slams pantries, leaves the fridge open and intentionally burns food so the smoke alarm goes off and wakes me up. You'd think that last instance I mentioned wouldn't be so common; however, Chloe had managed to pull that stunt that *three different times* since I'd gotten home from my weekend in Paris. I can tell something's bothering her, and her not knowing what that something is is killing her.

Meanwhile, I just stick to texting Hunter, practicing my music, and studying. It's all I've got to keep me from going insane from the wait. At night our texts get a little flirtatious. Hunter and I somehow manage to keep things PG-13. It's going to make his visit all the sweeter, I can tell. And I'm starting to get the sense that he likes me just as much as I like him. Which I'm not surprised to say is quite a lot.

I pop in One Night in Paris every once in a while. Really, it's every few days. It's such a sweet movie, it reminds me of Hunter. Of course, something in my gut tells me we're not going to see each other after this visit. After all, my semester abroad is coming to a close on the 30th, where I'll end up flying back to LA to finish my degree stateside. He's still got a year in his work-study program, and Hunter just might renew his contract for another year. He's really enjoying his time in Northern France, and who could blame him? I certainly can't. An ocean is going to separate us. We'll essentially be on opposite sides of the world in a little under a month's time. So we might as well enjoy the little time we do have together, right?

But, just as every other constant in life, time marches on. Or, as Hunter puts it: new movies always come out, and the old ones always find a way to get rediscovered.

The weekend of Hunter's planned visit arrives, and I find myself rushing to the airport to meet him in time for his landing. This friendship is far from old, but I'm ready to rediscover what brought us together in the first place.

I have a poster-board with his name written on it in permanent marker. He'll appreciate and hopefully laugh at the gesture. On the backside it reads "ANNIE", re-used from my last arrival in Berlin. Daisy and Samantha probably came up with the idea for that. I feel bad that they're caught in the cross-fire between Chloe and I. They don't deserve it. Daisy's cooled it with her one-liners. Samantha and I don't really talk anymore. I grip the sign tighter. It feels like it's all I have left of my friends. I pray that Hunter doesn't mind the sign. Hopefully it doesn't make me look like a penny-pincher or anything, but I doubt he'll even notice.

The cab arrives at the airport and I rush inside, suddenly forgetting to pay the cab driver, and I have to run back out to hand him the Euro I owed him. Hunter's in receiving, waiting, and I practically burst into the room waving the sign I made for him.

He's standing there, single-strapped backpack hoisted up over one shoulder casually supported by his hand, the other jammed deep in his pocket. He grins when I burst in, and I see his devilishly handsome smile one more time. My heart swells as he rushes over to me. We embrace, and I feel the warmth of his body pressed up against mine, reminding me of the slow dance we once shared under the Eiffel Tower. It feels so long ago, but his presence makes everything come back crystal-clear.

He looks down at me and I look up at him.

We kiss, making up for lost time. It's slow and passionate, and I can feel the warmth of his lips lighting a fire deep in my soul. My heart's about to burst. Hunter wraps an arm around my waist, the other holding my chin in place as he kisses me.

And just like that, it's over.

We pull back a little, but I've still got my arms wrapped around his neck affectionately. It's like we're practically a couple already. Hunter looks down at me and asks: "So, what took me so long?"

I laugh. "Your flight got delayed?"

"Some stewardess tried quitting mid-flight and they had to turn the plane around so she could leave. She couldn't just storm out of the office, after all."

"Did that really happen?"
Hunter laughs. "No, but can you imagine if it did?"

I giggle. "So, what should we do first?" Hunter looks around.

"We should probably get out of this airport, first and foremost."

We get in a cab together, splitting the cab fare back to my apartment. Hunter's going to stay with us, and unfortunately I forgot to mention this to Chloe beforehand. Daisy and Samantha won't care at all if Hunter sleeps on my floor. They've had plenty of houseguests before and we've never had conflict. But I just know Chloe's going to fly off the handle. And you know what? I'm actually looking forward to it. It'll give me a reason to clear the air between us.

On the cab ride back to my place, I brief Hunter again on what to expect from her. We're stopping by quickly just to drop his bags off, so hopefully the horn-locking conflict is kept to a minimum.

"So, she's crazy then?" Hunter's eyebrows cock. "Because to me, it sounds like she's crazy."

"Crazy in love. With me, I think," I add. "She's jealous of the amount of time you and I spend texting. She says I don't ever text her like that. Imagine how she's going to be once she sees us together. She's going to freaky freak out. You better be ready."

"Oh, *I'm ready.* She can bring it on. I'll one-up her craziness every. Single. Time." Hunter claps his hands between words, and I stifle a laugh, covering my mouth.

"Oh, you can laugh at that one, Annie. I mean it. You need to know that if I put on clown makeup and chase her around your apartment, that doesn't mean I care for you a single iota less. I'm doing it out of love, I swear." And we both laugh.

He's doing it out of love. Funny choice of words, there. What's even funnier is that I'm…I'm not fazed at all by it. Not one single iota.

The cab drives us through downtown Berlin, and around me I see grey skyscrapers, phone lines, and old metro tracks that run through the center of the city streets. It's not Paris, but it's home. Berlin's definitely grown on me since I've been here the past semester. It's not like L.A. one bit. I haven't seen a single palm tree, been harangued by any homeless people, or bumped into any wannabe actors.

Honestly, I kinda prefer Europe to the States. And I don't think I'm just saying that because Hunter's here. Life over here is just different, and that difference in lifestyle works really well for me. Public transit is in higher demand, I don't have to worry about medical bills, and the food here is a thousand and one times better than anything I'd ever eaten back home. I can't imagine how much it's going to suck when I leave. But I can't afford to think about that right now. I've got Hunter all to myself for another short weekend, and I don't plan on letting him go anytime soon.

The cab pulls up to my apartment and Daisy buzzes us in. I lead Hunter up the stairs and he playfully nudges me once we're just outside my door. *Here we go.*

"You ready?" he whispers to me. I nod, and unlock the front door. Chloe's inside, siting on the living room couch, phone in hand and texts flying invisibly through the air.

"Oh?" Chloe says, looking up at Hunter and I standing together in the doorway. "New friend?"

I nod. "New friend."

"So...*he's* the one you've been texting all this time, then? Wow. Can't say I'm surprised." Chloe shrugs and rolls her eyes just enough for us to see. She's back on her phone without giving us a chance to respond, so I guide Hunter past her and into my room where we can have some privacy.

"Wow, indeed," Hunter whispers once I've closed my door and he's set his backpack down. "Total. Wacko."

"I know, right?" My eyes widen once I figure Hunter finally understands what I've been telling him about her. "It's...been difficult lately. Honestly, it's been pretty hard living with her ever since I got back from Paris. Usually I can put up with her attitude, but it's getting to be too much lately. And it breaks my heart." I'm finding this difficult to brush off, but Hunter finds a way to try and make me feel better anyways.

"I think she's the worst. Worse than the worst, in fact. Doubly so."

I giggle, taking the edge off. "The worst of the worst won't accept her into their club because they just think she's the worst."

"The worst is yet to come. Or, in this case, the worst has *already* come and it's sitting in your living room."

We both laugh quietly, and I suggest we get out of here to avoid another Chloe encounter. Hunter nods.

"Lead the way."

Hunter and I walk through the Berlin streets as I point out the various spots I've spent my past semester hanging out in. I live in a neighborhood called *Mitte.* It's basically in the center of things here. I've got easy access to shopping, cafés and restaurants in just a short walk. The Reichstag—the one from the fire—is a few blocks away from my apartment.

We stop for schnitzel, and we both share a strudel with the most delicious cream you can imagine. It's like a fluffy white dollop of heaven. As I order the strudel, I ask the street vendor for one serving to share in a strange combination of English, French, and a little bit of German peppered in.

"Could we please...*posséder une*...strudel, *freuen?*"

Hunter and I share it as we lean over our hands, doing our best to catch all the scraps that fall to the sidewalk below. It's out of this world, and somehow even better when you're sharing it with someone you deeply care for. I can't explain it. Everything just tastes better that way.

I show Hunter around an old Opera House that still runs tours around the clock. We check out the old posters on the wall, featuring elegantly dressed women about to belt out the performance of their lives. The old opera stars had these long Italian- and Latin-sounding names. I can't pronounce any of them, but I can certainly appreciate their aesthetic.

Hunter sure thinks so, too, and asks me for a picture with some of the old posters and costumes on display. He makes a goofy grin and sticks both thumbs up when I take the picture, and it takes a lot for me not to laugh at his antics. He's just so charming when he's loosened up like this, and I resolve to never check my watch at all today, just so I can't feel the time pass when I've still got his company.

We leave the Opera House and start our long walk back to my apartment, agreeing on takeout on the way back home. There's a small hole-in-the-wall place just a few blocks south of my apartment, so we head there and Hunter orders more food for us than I could possibly eat in one sitting.

"This way, we have leftovers for the whole weekend!" and I then and there formally declare Hunter to be the smartest man that I'd ever met in the history of my life.

We manage to make it back to my place, where we eat the takeout on my bed as we sit cross-legged facing one another.

"So," I say between bites. "What do *you* want to do while you're in town?"

Hunter nods, stuffing his face with lo-mein. "Okay, I *did* want to try authentic sauerkraut while I'm here. And drink a huge beer from a stein. But that's about it."

"We can definitely arrange that for tomorrow. What about tonight?"

"How about a discotheque?" Hunter raises his eyebrows to gauge my response, and I nod.

"I could do a discotheque," I say. "I haven't been to one since I got here, and Daisy and Chloe both have this regular spot they go to…"

"Great," Hunter says. "Let's go there."

"What, now?"

"Yeah, now," Hunter takes my food, boxes it all up with his leftovers, and runs it out to our fridge in the kitchen. He pops back into my room and looks down at his outfit. He's wearing a button-down plaid shirt over a plain tee-shirt and jeans.

"You're going to need something a little more formal than that," I say.

"Good thing I brought a change of clothes, then."

I wonder if Hunter's going to change in here in front of me. He takes his shirt off in my bedroom, his back facing me. I turn away out of respect, but still turn around to take a peek. His back muscles are intense. I can tell he works out. Yep, he's hot, alright. He throws on a white-collar dress shirt that pair well with his khakis and formal shoes he's got tucked away in his bag. I throw a cute jacket over the blouse I'd been wearing. Fortunately the discotheque will let girls in wearing just about anything, the guys need to be dressed to the nines here, of course.

Hunter and I leave the apartment dressed sharply, and we decide to walk to the discotheque. Along the way we chat about this and that, and Hunter asks me what I'm going to do first when I get back to LA.

"Well, I think I'm going to find the greasiest hamburger I can possibly find, and then I'm going to stuff my face with it. How about you?"

"Huh. So, funny story."

"Yeah?"

"I don't think I want to go back to the U.S. Not anytime soon, at least."

I raise my eyebrows and look over at him. "Really? I mean, you did mention another year on the work study if you're applicable. But you *never* want to go back?"

Hunter shakes his head.

"Not really. I don't have much going for me back home. Here, I'm a stay-at-home caretaker. If I wanted to pursue it further, I could get a good live-in job with a client who can pay me handsomely. And I've got a good thing going now. My family, the Van der Meers, have a good thing going. Their villa overlooks this beautiful city square, and have I told you they take three-day weekends *every weekend?* That means *I* get a three-day weekend every weekend in the most beautiful little village you could ever ask for. Pretty soon I'll have enough saved up for my own place, and I can come and go as I please after work hours are over. So, no, I can't just leave. I've got a good thing going for me, one that'll possibly land me a solid career for me sometime soon. I'm sure you understand."

I nod. Of course I understand. But I don't say anything. Instead, we keep walking through the German city, passing by what feels like a million different people on our way to the discotheque. Hunter doesn't say anything after that. I'm sure he knows it's going to be difficult for us to see each other or even *talk* once I'm back home. We're going to be on a nine-hour time difference, at least. And that's not even mentioning the physical distance between us. With plane tickets costing two-thousand-plus dollars, it's going to be one hell of an occasion if either of us plan to fly out and see the other.

Of course, I say all this without even having asked Hunter if he'll *want* to see me again after this semester's ended. Who knows? I might just be a casual emotional fling for him. I sure hope that's not the case, but I silently prepare for the worst as we finally make it to the discotheque. The line's not too long, the bouncer lets us in as soon as we make it to the front after a few minutes wait.

Inside the club it's a whole other world. The bar sitting behind the dance floor is dimly lit with black lights, and the rest of the club is a strobe-light filled cacophony of electronica and horniness. Also, the whole place smells of beer. I'm used to that smell by now after living in Germany for a semester.

I'm shocked when Hunter takes my hand to guide me to the bar, but I grip his hand tight and follow along anyways. It's good to feel it again, his hand in mine. Hunter orders me a mojito, and he orders himself a dark German beer. Together we sip our drinks with our backs against the bar, looking out into the eccentric crowd dancing in front of us.

Hunter leans over to me and says something unintelligible. I can't hear a thing over this electronica music, and I have to lean over to shout at him to speak up.

"Do you want to find a table?!"

"Don't those cost money?!" I shout, needing to clarify before we're charged ten thousand Euro just to sit down in a club. Hunter shakes his head.

"I asked the bartender! He says we're good tonight unless some fat cat pounces on us! Come on!" and he takes my hand again and leads me through the crowd, our drinks still in hand as we navigate our way across the club. There's a row of booths just on the other side of the mosh pit that's forming at the heart of the dance floor, and Hunter and I manage to make it over there in one piece. We laugh, and I look down. We're still holding hands. It's the first time we've acknowledged the hand-holding part of our relationship. Hunter looks down at our hands, and then back to me.

"Want to hang around here for a while?!"

"Sure!" I grin, the electronica dubstep music still ringing in my ears. God, I'm going to go deaf because of this place. I don't normally go out to clubs, but Hunter being here and holding my

hand as we sit down in one of the empty booths really makes it all worth it. I'm not going to worry about whether or not he *really* wants to hold my hand, or if he's just asking to be polite. I'm not going to overthink things anymore. He asks me if I want to hang out, and I say yes. Total honesty.

We sit at the booth, our fingers interwoven between one another as we look into each other's eyes. Hunter's grinning ear to ear, and so am I. I can feel my face blushing, but I bet it's hard to see in the strobe lights. We can't really hear ourselves talk, so this club is honestly a perfect place for honeymooning couples who just want to stare into one another's eyes.

In this moment, my life is absolutely perfect.

Hunter finishes his beer and I down the rest of my mojito. It feels like we're ending all of our nights drinking, but I guess when in Rome, huh? At least it's common over here in Europe, I guess.

Hunter motions at my glass and cocks his eyebrows. Yeah, I'll take another drink. I nod gleefully as he gets up and heads back to the bar for another round. I sit and stare into my empty drink glass.

Despite all the loud noise I feel loose and free and more comfortable than ever before. Normally I have to keep my guard up when I go out with Chloe and the other girls. I've never been to a club, but even going out to dinner requires L.A. girls like me to keep on high alert. Watch out for creeps and toxic friends wanting to start drama, that sort of thing. But with Hunter, I'm free to do and feel as I please. He's not going to judge anything I do. I'm safe with him. He'll keep me safe. He's the sweetest, kindest person I've ever met. Plus, he's pretty darn cute, too. Did I mention that part?

He's back with our drinks, and I practically snatch the mojito from his hands and chug half of it in one go. Hunter starts to laugh, and he sits down and chugs his beer, too. Only he's able to down the entire glass in one fell swoop, and he leans back and belches once the glass is completely free of any suds. I can hear his burp from here, even the club can't drown that one out. I laugh and give him a thumbs up, and Hunter leans back in his seat, proud of his work.

I keep drinking my mojito and look around at the people dancing and lurching all around us. It looks like there's a million people all crammed in here, pressed up tightly against one another's bodies. The floor's wet, probably all from alcohol, puke and sweat that's collectively dripping from everyone's forehead. There's probably spit mixed in there, too. Boy, is it *hot* in here. I feel a wave of heat coming from the mosh pit that's been building up on the dance floor. Everyone's dressed to the nines, Hunter looks like he's in casual clothes compared to everyone else here. I look like a pretty typical German girl. I do well to blend in a crowd. Blouses are in at the moment, and I don't look out of place here at all. I think Hunter looks dapper, leaning back there in the booth, proud of his chugging abilities. It's not everyday you get to see someone you care about down an entire sixteen ounce glass of beer in less than ten seconds. I can't really explain it, but everything he does now is just *so* attractive.

Then, he offers me his hand and I accept it. We get up, take our empty drink glasses to the bar as a courtesy and head out to the dance floor.

We join the mosh pit, Hunter keeping as close as possible to me. I can see the top button of his shirt's unbuttoned now, and I get a glimpse of his chest. I put one hand around his shoulders and lean in close to him as we dance energetically to the beat of the discotheque. Around us everyone else is caught up in the groove, too, and I feel like I could stay here for a million years.

For a moment, we lock eyes and I think we're about to kiss again. But we don't, and Hunter ends up laughing and bowing out of the dance floor early. I follow him curiously.

"*You tired?!*" he shouts and I nod.

Hunter gives me a nod, pointing toward the door from which we came in, and I nod in agreement. Let's bounce. We end up dipping out from the front entrance past the bouncer and into the street. Boy, I'm drunk. Hunter is, too.

He immediately motions to the busy part of the street. "Cab?"

"Cab," I slur, nodding my head sloppily.

We head close to the square where cars pull in and out, dropping passengers off and picking new ones up. The cars here are just the most elegant ones I've ever seen. I don't know the names of any of the models, but they all look fancier than a Rolls-Royce and Mercedes-Benz combined into one supercar. I guess the Germans really *are* known for their cars.

Hunter manages to flag down a cab, and we lurch inside as Hunter goes in first. I follow him in after, and I slip and manage to land face-first in his lap as we both giggle drunkenly. The cabbie doesn't seem to mind how intoxicated we are, and I slur my apartment's address up at him before leaning back over to Hunter and laughing.

The cab ride back is all a blur. At some point, Hunter grabs my hand again. Our fingers stay interlocked as we pay the cabbie with an extra large tip and step back out onto the sidewalk. I lead the way back up to my apartment, and before I know it we're in my bedroom. Hunter closes the door behind me and motions to the floor.

"Any place in particular I should sleep? And don't you dare offer me the couch," he slurs. "I'm not going to wake up to a hot mess of Chloe all in my face. No way," and we both laugh at that.

"No, no. Just—just sleep in my bed," I offer. "There's—*hic*—plenty of room for the both of us. *I promise*," I whisper in his ear, leaning onto his shoulder. Hunter belches, covering his mouth, and then he laughs again. I guess I *do* have game, after all.

I flick off the light, but I can still see him through the outline of the dark. I watch as Hunter unbuttons his shirt, and for the first time I can see he's got muscles tapered onto that skinny frame of his. He's got a nice chest with pecs I just want to lay my hand on instinctively. It takes a lot of self-control not to. I decide I might as well undress, too. I remove my blouse, slip my bra off when I've got a baggy tee-shirt over it, and take off my pants. Hunter does so, too, and before we know it we're both in my bed.

Hunter looks over to me and smiles. I smile back.

He leans over, and we kiss.

His lips are as firm as I imagined them, yet somehow still soft as well. He brings his hand up to the back of my head, holding me in place. If I were standing, my legs would turn to jelly. We keep on kissing, with each smooch growing more and more passionate. I want more and more from him, and I can feel that he wants the same from me.

We pull back suddenly, and Hunter and I both lock eyes for the briefest of moments. His eyes are dark with lust, and his lips dry from the sweaty club. I just want to kiss them, to moisten them up. I feel a million tiny needles in my chest prick with excitement. I just want to grab him, kiss him, tell him how much he means to me.

Hunter kisses me again, and I know it's on.

He rolls on top of me, and we get back to kissing. Things grow hotter and heavier, and before I know it I can feel his hand on my chest. It's gentle, yet firm, and I feel myself getting more and more excited as he kisses me ever so passionately.

We spend the entire night making love and whispering each other's names into our ears. It's a beautiful, sweaty, romantic blur.

Once it's done, I fall asleep with my head resting on Hunter's chest. Nothing could be more perfect than this moment, half-awake, half-asleep, holding someone I truly love.

CHAPTER EIGHT

We awake pretty late into the morning hour to the sound of Chloe banging around in the kitchen. She's practically banging pots and pans together, and I feel my stomach sink as I figure that she probably heard Hunter and I coming home late last night. Somewhere she's blasting music, and I find the annoying dancehall beat is not nearly as charming as it was last night in the club. My stomach turns into a knot. We probably made a lot of noise coming home, and then…Chloe probably heard us last night, alright. I figure Daisy and Samantha are annoyed by her antics, too, but this conflict is between me and her. They can put on headphones. That's how it's going to be.

I'm yanked out of my half-groggy thoughts suddenly. Chloe drops a glass on the floor and I hear the pieces tinkling everywhere as she squeals in dismay. I'm not freaking out on her for that one. I get it. Accidents happen.

Not even three seconds later, another glass smashes. This time, Chloe laughs, and I assume this one is done on purpose. I take back any shred of regret I may have felt for my actions.

I get up, throw on some sweatpants and a sweatshirt before looking back at Hunter, who's still passed out in my bed. He's sprawled out, one arm under his head as he smiles in his sleep. I hope he's dreaming about me. I put on Hunter's button down shirt, buttoning it loosely as I leave my room.

I go out past the living room and into the kitchen where Chloe's making her daily ruckus to spite me. She's got music blaring from her phone, alright, and she's got a million plates and pots out just to make a simple plate of spaghetti. At ten in the morning, no less. Chloe isn't the worst cook in the world, but she certainly is in the running for second or third place.

"Can you keep it down in here?" I wince at the sunlight emanating from the window. "Still trying to sleep here."

"Oh, I'm sorry. Did I wake you?" Chloe feigns worry, and I instantly regret any concern I may have felt for her. "I should have asked first before making a ruckus. I'm sorry about that, Annie, I truly am." I can tell she's not, but I instantly know what she's getting at.

"Yeah, uh, sorry about last night," I shrug, scratching an itch on the back of my neck. Chloe's not buying it, however, and she tries to grill me as I stand there half-asleep in the kitchen. She's got a pot of water boiling, and there's another pan with sauce that I can tell has already burnt beyond edibility.

"So, he's still here, then?"

I nod.

"Hunter?"

I nod again. There's no escaping this. I'm not going to make Hunter climb out the window from a rope made of bedsheets. She might as well know the truth that's sleeping in the other room.

"Well, well. So there *is* something there. Tell me *everything*," Chloe says, eager to gossip. I figure she's going to go behind my back later to smack-talk me to Daisy and Samantha, it's only natural. So I elect to keep my mouth shut. I shake my head, and Chloe sighs. Sure, Daisy and Samantha don't *want* to gossip about me, but Chloe can be pretty imposing at times. She likes a captive audience. And one that listens to her every order, which I'm failing to do.

"Well, fine. Have it your way, then," she resigns. "It's not like we're roommates or anything. And I've been meaning to ask you: how *do* you think we ended up together here in Berlin? Have you ever given any thought to how we of all people ended up as roommates after years of not seeing one another?"

I shake my head. I *hadn't* thought about it, if I'm being honest.

"That's because I pulled some strings, had my parents cash in some favors from my school. I *asked* about you. I asked that we lived together. And look where that's gotten me. Whatever."

I'm shocked to the core with the news. So Chloe's the reason we've been living together. She asked about me, had us live to-gether after pulling in some favors. I can't believe how selfish I'd been. I can't believe myself.

Chloe looks back to the pot of water that's now boiling over and spilling out onto the countertop, and she scrambles to throw in her pasta noodles. I leave her to her cooking and go back to my bedroom, shaken with the news of her manipulation.

She's the reason we're living together, and I'm ruining everything.

Hunter's awake now, sitting up and rubbing his eyes.

"She wake you, too, then?" he asks groggily, and I nod.

"It's a habit of hers. A bad one, I should say." I plop back down on the bed next to Hunter, who's now scrolling through a social media page on his phone, half-awake. "Wake me when she's fin-ished," I mumble into the pillows.

"Uh, I'm going to jump out the window before I see *her* again," Hunter says. "She's a bitch, just like you said."

I sit up, suddenly red-hot with an anger and frustration I never thought Hunter could make me feel. "Don't say that. I never said she was a bitch, don't try to put words in my mouth. And, Hunter, we did come home pretty late last night. We both know how much noise we made."

Hunter shrugs. "Chloe's still a terrible person. I don't feel bad at all for what we did. You better not either."

I find myself more upset over his words than Chloe's actions.

"Hey, hang on a minute. You're the guest here. This is technic-ally *her* apartment, too, you know." But Hunter just shrugs again and goes back to scrolling on his phone. I can't *stand* the indiffer-ence. I hate it when Chloe does this to me, and it's even more hurt-ful when Hunter acts this way. Especially after last night.

"Hey, look at me. We need to talk."

Hunter puts his phone down, looking dumbfounded.

"You can't talk about her that way anymore. Seriously." Hunter just looks puzzled, cocking an eyebrow as he raises his voice in protest.

"Hey, you said those words about her yourself, you know. I'm just repeating what you said. If you don't like it, maybe I should leave."

I cross my arms as Hunter gets out of my bed and dresses quickly. He's buttoning up his shirt from last night, throws his pants on and ties his shoes efficiently. He's ready to go in thirty seconds.

"See you around," he says, looking down at the floor. I sigh, unable to look at him.

"See you around."

And with that, Hunter is out the door.

CHAPTER NINE

My semester abroad ends in heartbreak. Hunter leaves Berlin without speaking to me at all. I don't text him, and he doesn't text me. I assume things have ended between us, as I've only got a few short weeks left before I'm to head back to LA for good and there's no way we can fit in an in-person apology.

I pass all my finals. I wasn't too worried about them, and after Hunter leaving I was able to cram a lot more studying in before all my tests. It helped me take my mind off of him, anyways. I'm sure he was doing the same with his work-study. Probably put in more hours just to clear his head. I wouldn't blame him at all, and with each passing day I find myself regretting my actions more and more. He was right. Chloe was being super shitty that morning. I don't know why I defended her.

After that morning, Chloe didn't warm up to me any more than she already had before. I took a stand, defending her honor against Hunter's insistence that she was terrible, and it blew up in my face entirely. We don't speak for the final few weeks of our stay. We pass each other in the hallway between the kitchen and the living room, exchanging a few "excuse me's" here and there, but that's it. Chloe goes back to banging her pots and pans around every morning, but I've lost the energy to confront her on it anymore. I know it'll just break my heart regardless.

I dumped Hunter for Chloe, and she's giving me the cold shoulder, too. I just can't win.

Eventually, December 30th rolls around, breezing by Christmas Day like it was nothing. Chloe, Daisy and Samantha all exchanged gifts that day, and I just hung out in my room, watching movies. It was all I could do to stop from breaking down in tears. But that day, just like every other, ended, and I was left to finish the semester in isolation. I took myself to the Berlin Tegel Airport on the morning of the 30th, and boarded my flight without any issue.

The plane landed in Los Angeles almost twelve hours later, my Dad waiting for me at the airport. His kind face hasn't aged a day, but the hair loss he'd been dealing with before I left escalated to the point where his head is now shaved. I can get used to it. It makes him look all the more dignified with his pure-white goatee. When I arrive in the receiving area, Dad smiles and hugs me tight, pressing me close against his denim jacket that smelled of gasoline. Long day at work, I guess. He'd been a gas station manager for the past twenty years after his acting career never took off, but that didn't stop him from loving me any less. It's just been a little harder ever since Mom left, that's all.

"You ready to be home?" Dad asks me after our hug. I nod, doing my best not to cry after all the heartbreak at the end of my semester. "Let's get you home then. Still want that burger you were texting me about?"

Dad takes me to my favorite burger place, Greasy Heaven, and it's there where I can finally enjoy my greaseball American cheeseburger, just the way I missed them. Dad and I eat in the car in the parking lot, a paper bag of trash sitting between us as we share an order of french fries.

"So, what was the best part?"

I shrug. "Best part?"

Dad's in shock. "Of your semester? You know, the one you just had in Europe? What was the best part?"

It was Hunter. "I don't really know, Dad. I don't want to talk about it right now."

Dad sets his burger down. He's obviously upset, which I completely understand considering he helped pay for my flight to and from Germany. "Tell me something good that happened, then, Annie. Anything."

But I just shake my head. "Dad, I really don't want to talk about it right now." I try changing the subject. "Tell me about your store. How's it going over there with the new staff?"

And now it's Dad's turn to shake his head. "Shitty, if I'm being honest. Terrible, even. They can't work together as a team to save their own jobs. If I tell one of my staff members to do something, the buck gets passed around until *I'm* the one that ends up doing the task out of...*sheer frustration*." Dad clenches his teeth, and I can tell he's already stressed just from thinking about things. "That's why I want to hear about your semester, Annie. Work's been shitty, and I just need to hear that all that hard work I did was worth it. All that hard work you did, too. You passed your finals, right?"

I nod. "Yeah, I passed. And I had fun, Dad. It just got rough at the end."

"How so?"

"You remember Chloe. We got into a big fight at the end and never made up."

Dad scoffs. "You two, always bickering over this or that. You know, I really can't tell if you two are even friends to begin with. *Are* you two even really friends?"

I pause. I don't know. I genuinely don't know the answer.

"If you have to think about it that long, then you aren't," Dad finishes my thought for me.

I sigh. "Also, there was a boy."

Dad raises an eyebrow and turns to look at me. "Explain."

And I tell him all about Hunter. Well, mostly everything. I tell him about our meeting in Paris, how we clicked instantly the moment we met. Our dance under the Eiffel Tower. The meetup in Berlin, and the date to the discotheque. I leave out the part in my bed, of course, but everything else is one hundred percent the truth. The whole while Dad listens pensively, nodding every few seconds, never breaking eye contact. He's a great listener, and I feel myself pouring out feelings I didn't know I had.

After I finish, Dad just sighs and leans back into his chair, staring out the window.

"Dad?"

"Hang on, Annie. I'm thinking."

We sit there for a few minutes in utter silence. I finish my burger slowly, wondering what Dad's thinking right now. When he finally speaks up, it's in a quiet tone, and I know what he's saying is one hundred per cent serious.

"Annie, it sounds like that boy did right by you."

I nod and look out the window. I can already tell where this is going.

"And it sounds like he cares about you a lot."

"*Cared,*" I correct him. "Cared. Past tense."

"No, to me it sounds like he *cares*, present tense. You told him to leave and he immediately obliged you. No muss, no fuss. Annie, let me tell you this: if you tell a guy to leave and he argues with you, he likes you. Heck, he may have feelings for you. But if you tell a guy to leave, and he does it in a minute? Honey, he either hates you or he loves you, and I don't think that boy hates you one single iota. He's probably letting you cool off. That's how your Mom and I handled things. Well, that's not the best example to draw from, but you get the picture. No, I don't think he's mad at you at all. He probably thinks you hate his guts."

I feel hot tears welling up. I know Dad's right. He always is when it comes to these sorts of things.

"So, what do I do?"

"You've got his number, right? Call him!"

And I pull out my phone, looking at Dad for confirmation. Dad nods, and I step out of the car into the hot California mid-afternoon, dialing Hunter's number.

CHAPTER TEN

Hunter picks up on the first ring.

"Hello?" he sounds groggy and tired, and I suddenly realize that he's still on European time. It's the middle of the night over there. I wonder if he's staying up late, waiting for me to call him. I doubt it, but the picture in my mind makes me feel better about my call. For one brief moment, I consider hanging up without saying a word, but I know Dad will just ask me about it anyways.

"Hunter?"

"Yeah?"

"I'm sorry. About last time we saw each other. About Chloe. You were right, she was being shitty. I was wrong."

Hunter sighs, and I hear his tiredness creeping out. He'd rather be asleep than talking to me. I probably woke him up. He's probably with another girl right now, probably about to—

"Are you alone?" I ask him.

"Yeah," he says. "I'm alone. I haven't...haven't seen anyone since you. I don't really want to, either."

"What do you mean?"

Hunter pauses. "I mean exactly that. I haven't seen, or wanted to see, anyone since you kicked me out. I don't know, I just...you know?"

I nod, then realize Hunter isn't here to pick up on my non-verbal cues. "Yeah, I know. Me too, by the way. About the alone thing, I mean." *Gosh, could I <u>sound</u> more desperate and lonely?*

Hunter doesn't seem to notice, however. "Okay," he says.

"Will I ever see you again?"

"If you're ever back over here again, absolutely," Hunter says. "You have my word."

I smile. "Thanks."

"Be seeing you," Hunter says. "I need to get some sleep. Big day at work tomorrow."

"Yeah," I say. "Goodnight, Hunter."

"Goodnight," he says, and hangs up.

I look back at Dad, still in the car, and give him a thumbs up.

For the next three months, I help Dad out at the gas station. I pick up the slack that his staff leaves behind, and soon Dad and I are working together to manage the competent employees that stick around. We're a team, Dad and I. I can't believe how happy I feel working with him. Life goes back to normal. I re-enroll in college back home, but elect to take all my classes online. Gives me more time to work that way, and works keeps my mind off of things. Yeah, I'm happy here, but I know I'd be happier with Hunter. And that's just the truth.

Works keeps my mind off of Hunter, I mean. Sure, we made up, but I still haven't been able to *see* him. To tell him I'm sorry in person is the only way I can make sure things are right between us. And I want to see him again anyways, outside of apologizing.

One day, I send Hunter a short text.

"Hey, hope the work-study hasn't killed you yet. :)"

He replies back early the next afternoon, I assume when he's about to go to bed.

"Oh, you know, just normal murderous work. How's home?"

"Same old, same old. Thinking about flying back over to the old E.U. if you'll see me. Just gotta save up that flight money."

Hunter doesn't respond for a while, which makes me nervous. Eventually, he replies:

"Come on over whenever. We can kiss and make up in person when you get here."

I like the sound of that quite a bit, and I put my everything into saving every penny I can.

Another two months of work and I've managed to save up enough for a ticket. One-way flight to Paris. A single layover in Pittsburgh, then I take a train from Paris to Fourcés where Hunter's at.

Dad drives me to the airport and we don't say anything for the whole ride there. When I get out of the car to leave, Dad stops me.

"Annie, make it right. Come home whenever you want to. You've got my blessing."

I smile, wave goodbye to Dad, and head into the airport to board my plane. It's hard leaving Dad behind again, but we both know it's to pursue real happiness. Dad's going to be okay without me. Plus, we'll keep in touch while I'm across the pond.

I head to my gate with my head up, optimistic for the future.

Hunter greets me at the bus station when I get off in Fourcés. He's put on some weight. Muscle mass, I mean, by the looks of it. He's grinning ear-to-ear when I step off the bus, and I can tell immediately that there's no bad blood.

He embraces me and we kiss as soon as we're in each other's close proximity.

"I missed you," Hunter says.

"I missed you too," I grin.

Hunter takes me to his villa he's been staying at for the past two years now. It's a cute little place, just uptown. This place is about four hours north of Paris by train. It's small enough for a population of a few thousand, at least.

Hunter's family villa is a super-nice place, and Hunter says we can stay there as long as we like. He's got his own mini guesthouse, separated entirely from the main house the Van der Meers stay in. Hunter says I can stay here as long as I like and the Van der Meers won't mind it at all. Heck, they probably won't even notice I'm here. It's cozy, enough room for the both of us to reside peacefully with our own private spaces to relax. I've got my backpack and a suitcase full of clothes, with no end date in sight to my visit.

All I have to do is log in every once in a while to my school online to turn in homework, but that's it. I can focus on my music full-time. I brought my ukulele, so I've got something to work with here.

Hunter and I get to see each other every night. We slow dance by the fire when we can. He always tells me about his day, and I always catch him up to speed on my music. Maybe one day I can put together an album, sell it online, help out with the bills when Hunter's got a place of his own that we can move into. But for now, Hunter's got things covered. He insisted so himself, telling me that my company is more than enough. He always knows how to reassure me and keep me steady. I won't have to leave if I don't want to. Hunter makes enough from his work study to pay a mortgage on the villa, and he'll own it in just a few short years. He's going to have a job lined up for him when he graduates. Maybe I'll look into getting a job out here, too. Hunter says I can stay with him for as long as I like, and he hopes that I'll never leave. I tell him I'm here for good, as long as he'll have me.

One day, a few weeks into my visit, Hunter comes home with a comically large smile plastered upon his face. I've been here no longer than a month. I'm sitting on the loveseat in the main living room, gazing out the window as I strum a chord aimlessly.

"Annie?"

"What?" I ask, looking up from my ukulele. He's holding something behind his back.

"I got us a hotel for the weekend. We can get away, take a nice little trip. No work, no music, but only if you don't want to work on it. Just you and me. What do you say?"

"And where would this majestic weekend away take place, do tell?"

Hunter grins. "Why, Paris, of course."

Where else?

We spend our weekend together in a hotel overlooking the Eiffel Tower and the adjacent park. The park where we shared our first slow dance. Now, we share our slow dances by a fireplace at night, but the warm fuzzy sentiment is always there.

We take a day trip to the Louvre, taking our time to soak in all the art around the gallery. We don't check out the Mona Lisa at all. Hunter thinks it's overrated, too. One painting catches my eye, and I call Hunter over to check it out. It's Velasquez's *Las Meninas* again. I can just see myself in every subject painted.

The little girl with her head cocked to one side, refusing to accept the life that's bestowed upon her. Maybe she'll grow up and go on an adventure, far from home, where she can experience life to the fullest. I don't know what I'm supposed to get out of this painting, but I know I feel *something* looking at it. Maybe it's a feeling of hope. Maybe I can read sentiments and feelings into things that don't exist. Whatever it is, I love the painting, and Hunter buys us a copy to hang up in the living room when we get home. That Velasquez really did know his stuff.

On our walk back from the Louvre, Hunter takes me to a familiar spot. It's the bridge we walked over countless times before, the one with all the locks on the fences. Hunter pulls something out of his pocket to show me.

It's a lock with the key still inserted.

"I got this for us," he says. "Want to do the honors?"

I smile. Hunter's got a permanent marker in his jacket pocket, and he hands the lock and the marker to me. I write our initials on the front of the lock, circling them together in a perfect heart shape.

Hunter unlocks the lock once I've finished, and clips it to the fence overlooking the River Seine. He clicks it shut, pulls out the key, and hands it to me.

"Your call."

I kiss the key and throw it into the river below. The lock will stay here forever, hopefully. But there's no second guessing that our love will remain eternal.

Hunter and I go back to the hotel, back to spending the rest of our lives together. He takes my hand and holds it tight. I gaze up at the Eiffel Tower as we pass it by, a symbol of a city and a love that will never leave us for as long as we live.

THE END.

SIGN UP FOR MY MAILING LIST AND RECEIVE A FREE ROMANTIC SHORT!

Sign up to receive email notifications when new shorts, novellas and novels are released to Amazon, and receive a FREE copy of my romantic short, "My Dinner with the Devil", not available anywhere else!

Follow the link below to sign up!

http://eepurl.com/gSJrE1

BOOKS BY THIS AUTHOR

A Face In The Crowd

A rockstar fifteen years past his prime. An up-and-coming young DJ about to take the electronica scene by storm. Together they will change the music industry...but can they make a relationship work between the two of them?

Roland Biggs was the biggest thing in music--thirty years ago, to be precise. And he's experiencing the worst slump he's ever had at the end of a pretty prolonged career death. His agent offers him one last chance to get his career back up and running at the Old & New Tour, and he reluctantly accepts the offer.

Jane Parker is about to change the DJ scene forever. She's bouncing from club to club, putting literary references galore in her music and jumps at the chance to perform at the Old & New Tour.

Together Roland and Jane must work past their musical differences and see what they truly mean to one another. Strong language and mature themes. NO CHEATING, SAFE, HEA STORY!

Heartbreaker's Contract: A Billionaire's Fake Fiancée Standalone

Five years together. A fake wedding, a fake divorce, a fake everything. But the paycheck he's offering is very real...

This was supposed to be my dream job. Personal assistant to

Shane Lockwood. Yes, that Shane Lockwood. The billionaire cut-throat sports agent who's got a new supermodel on his arm every week and an endless list of world-famous athletes as his clients. But his career is stagnating, Shane tells me. And the only thing that can save it is a plan involving a publicized fake marriage to a fake fiancée.

The phony fiancée he has in mind?

Me.

When he hands me the contract detailing our agreement, our fingers touch, an electric heat pulsing down to my core. I can't stop staring at his dark, lustrous eyes, his broad shoulders and strong arms, his concealed muscles sculpted to perfection.

All he needs is my signature. This jerk will own my life for the next five years, but I'll be paid handsomely, making me richer than even my wildest dreams.

I sign.

The ink's still wet when I realize that I have no idea who the real Shane Lockwood is. That's something he keeps behind a cold steel wall--and doesn't let anyone inside.

When a crisis strikes our office, Shane makes me choose between two equally undesirable outcomes when we're forced to collect a client's unpaid debt. And now I've got to get his business and our wedding planning sorted out before the heartbreaker rips our contract in two.

But he's not the only one who can cut a deal. I know my way around the block, I can play his game too...and I just might have a shot at winning.

Heartbreaker's Contract is a STEAMY 55k Romance with a HEA and can be read as a standalone with no cliffhanger. Snag your copy today!

www.ingramcontent.com/pod-product-compliance
Lightning Source LLC
Chambersburg PA
CBHW020500160726
47991CB00007B/2743